SHARON GOSLING

THE HOUSE OF HIDDEN WONDERS

LiTTLE TiGER
LONDON

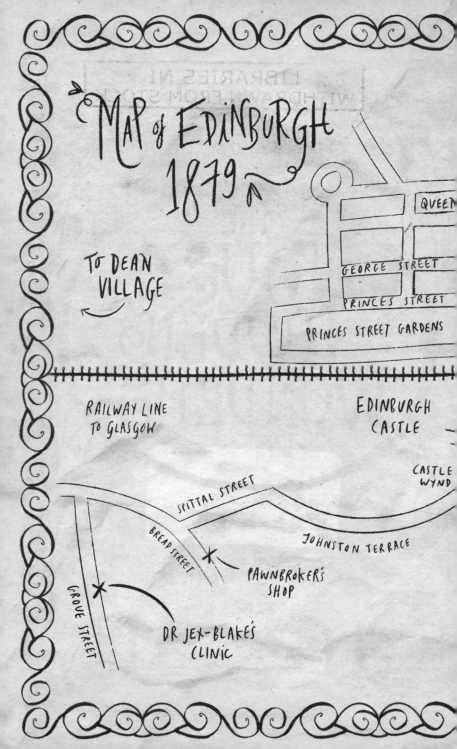

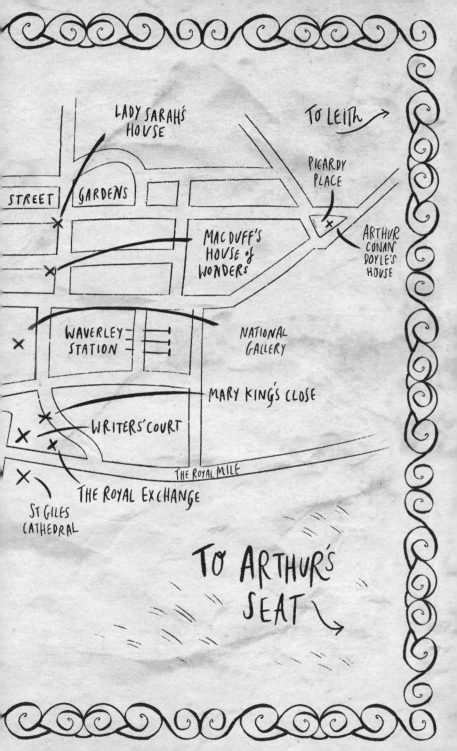

~PROLOGUE~

The ghost and her demon move in silence, hidden by shadows, cloaked in night. Down the long columns of darkness they drift: unseen, unheard. The rain does not touch them, neither does the chill wind. Despite the hour, the streets are busy, but no one notices them. No one calls after them or points them out. They are as invisible as the silver moon once hidden behind a storm cloud.

The ghost keeps moving. This place is not dark enough for her, nor the one after, nor even the next or the next. She has no home, nowhere to rest. She wanders, seeking; a restless spirit. There is no place where she belongs.

Somewhere behind her a great clock strikes twelve, its bell clanging into the gloom. It is midnight. The witching hour. The time when spirits rise. Her demon chatters, then quiets. A crack appears in the darkness beside her:

a passageway to the underworld. The ghost and her demon float in, and on, on, on.

Way down deep they go, then deeper still, into the midnight dark.

CHAPTER 1

"Run!" Zinnie shouted over her shoulder.

"He'll never catch us!" Nell shouted back, as she dithered after Zinnie. "He ain't got a chance!"

"Stop messing about, Nell!" Zinnie ordered her little sister. "Just *run*! Sadie, you too!"

She could hear their footsteps thundering behind her as they fled through the twilight. High above their heads the castle loomed, the yellow sandstone of its slabs turning black in the setting sun. She jinked a sharp left and there ahead were the steps of Castle Wynd. Zinnie glanced behind her. Sadie still looked fresh but Nell was puffing hard, beads of sweat gleaming on her forehead. Zinnie frowned. It wasn't like Nell to be slow – usually, her feet were as quick as her tongue. Further behind she could see the lawman gaining on them.

We won't make it, Zinnie thought, trying to catch her breath. *Not like this.*

She paused, letting Sadie and Nell pass her. As they did, Zinnie hooked the silver watch out of her pocket and slipped it into the fold of Nell's grubby pinafore.

"Keep going," she told them. "Don't look back. Split up in the market and hide. Don't go straight home – he might follow."

"What about you?" Sadie cried.

"I'll be right behind you – go!"

Sadie grabbed Nell's hand and pulled her up the steps, taking them two at a time. Zinnie followed, but slowly, making sure the constable had her in his sights. When he came puffing on to the steps, she faked a stumble, as if she'd slipped and fallen. She tugged her cap down lower over her eyes, stayed down for a beat, two, waiting until he was almost level with her…

"You, boy," the policeman called weakly, wheezing his way up the steps, his cheeks red with the effort of the chase. "Stop in the name of the law. I—"

Zinnie kicked out with her foot, catching his ankle just hard enough that he buckled to his knees with an '*oof!*' Then she was away, streaking up the worn stone steps, dodging in and out of the shadows and around curious onlookers until she'd reached the top.

"You!" the copper cried, still trying to regain his footing. "I'll get you yet, you little scoundrel! I'll—"

Zinnie made a show of turning left, but once she knew she was hidden among the knots of people that still crowded the thoroughfare she dashed right, down Castlehill towards the High Street. The sun had dropped below the horizon now, but there was still a faint glow in the air, even with the heavy blur of rain clouds gathering overhead. The late stalls were out, selling the leftover scraps that only the desperate would buy. This was Old Edinburgh. There were a lot of desperate people here.

"Zinnie!"

Sadie was peeking out from the shadows of St Giles. Zinnie looked around but there was no sign of the policeman. He'd not find them now, not in this crowd.

"Are you all right?" Sadie asked, as Zinnie reached her.

"Fine," Zinnie said. "Where's Nell?"

Sadie shook her head. "Don't know. She'll hide somewhere for a bit. You did say..."

Zinnie nodded. "All right. She's got the watch, though. If I take it to him now, we might be able to afford some supper."

Just the thought of food made her stomach rumble. There hadn't been enough bread for them all to eat that morning, so Zinnie had given Nell her own share. Now though, hunger gnawed at Zinnie's empty insides like a sharp-toothed rat.

"Come on," said Sadie. "He's long given up. Let's go home."

They'd only got as far as the entrance of Writers' Court when they spotted Nell further down the whip-thin street. She had her back against the wall, staring up at the man looming over her.

"That's Bartholomew Talbot!" Sadie hissed.

Despite herself, Zinnie's heart turned over. *Bartholomew Talbot.* A terrible, cruel man. She usually tried to stay as far away from him as possible. But she couldn't let him hurt Nell.

"Talbot," Zinnie said, running up to step between him and Nell. "What do you want?"

"What's it to you?"

"You don't mess with my sisters. You should know that by now."

Talbot's face twisted into a sneer as his gaze flicked between Nell and Zinnie. "Sister?" he said. "I don't think so."

Zinnie lifted her chin so she could look him in the eye. She slipped her fingers into her pocket and pulled out her knife, flicking it open without looking away. "Let her *go*."

Talbot narrowed his eyes. "I think you've got a death wish, girlie, threatening me with that little trinket. I was just asking your *sister* a polite question, is all. About that wee glint of silver I can see in her pocket there. Got a notion it ain't hers, see."

"It's not," Zinnie agreed. "But it isn't yours, either, and I'm about to make sure it gets back to its rightful owner.

Bet that's not something you'd do, is it? In fact, I wouldn't be surprised if it were you that nicked it from the gent who's missing it in the first place."

Talbot smiled again, but his eyes were as cruel as ever. "You'd best be careful, my wee lambs. Watch yourselves, all right?"

He turned and jerked his head. One by one, four big men slid out of the shadows to flank him. Talbot gave Nell a rot-toothed grin. Then he and his cronies were gone, barging their way through the bustle on the Royal Mile.

"Oh!" said Nell, throwing her arms round Zinnie's waist and almost knocking her over. "I'll never be as brave as you, Zinnie! I'll never be able to stand up to Talbot like you do!"

Zinnie snapped her knife closed and put it back in her pocket before hugging Nell.

"I'd rather you never saw him again," she said. "But if you do, there's no shame in running away, pippin. I'd rather you do that than ever face the likes of Bartholomew Talbot alone. You see him coming, you run. All right?"

"All right," said Nell, and then began to cough.

"Nell?" Sadie asked with a frown.

"It's just the running, that's all."

Sadie pressed a hand to Nell's forehead. "You're hot."

Nell huffed. "Course I am! You pulled me up those steps so quickly I thought I was flying!"

Zinnie retrieved the watch from Nell's pocket. "Take her home," she told Sadie. "I'll get rid of this and be back with something for us all to eat before you know it."

Sadie nodded and took Nell's hand. Zinnie watched them go, then turned down the Mile, making for the curving turn of Cockburn Street and the elegant squares of the New Town beyond.

CHAPTER 2

"Miss Zinnie!" exclaimed Arthur Conan Doyle, standing in the centre of his study with the silver watch she'd just given him dangling from his hand like a pendulum.

"Just Zinnie is fine," Zinnie told him.

"It would be impolite for me to be so familiar," the young man declared. "Now tell me – *how*? From where did you retrieve it?"

Zinnie shrugged. She was hardly going to tell him that they'd had to steal it from the window of a pawnbroker's shop. "It doesn't matter."

Conan Doyle shook his head. "Well, thank you. This will mean a great deal to the friend from whom it was stolen. He thought never to see it again. I confess, I feared that this time I must surely have given you a task that would confound even your skills. I am glad to have been mistaken."

Every now and then, Arthur Conan Doyle asked Zinnie to find something for him, usually something that had been lost or stolen. The watch had been his latest request – although he'd actually referred to it as 'the Pursuit of the Purloined Pocket Watch'.

"And now," he said, "let me find you and those sisters of yours something for your trouble."

Conan Doyle turned away to his desk, which gave Zinnie a chance to look round the room. She'd never been inside his house on Picardy Place before, much less into his study. Usually, he came to find her on the Mile, or talked to her briefly out in the hallway. But it seemed that by returning the purloined pocket watch Zinnie had proven something to Conan Doyle. That she was trustworthy perhaps. Zinnie didn't really care as long as he kept finding work for her to do.

The study looked out over the street via a large bow window. There was a desk and a fireplace, a chair, tables and … books. Books everywhere, on shelves and in stacks on the tables, the chairs, even on the floor. Several were open on the desk, along with a folded newspaper, a notebook and an ink pen, as if he'd just been sitting there, taking notes.

Conan Doyle opened one of the desk drawers, pulling out a little leather money pouch and upending it into his palm. From the pile of coins he took a half-crown and held it out to her. It was the most money Zinnie had seen in a long time and she took it quickly, clenching it in her fist as if it might vanish. Forget just supper – this would keep them fed for days without even having to beg. Zinnie was careful not to show Conan Doyle just how much the money meant to her, though. She had no intention of being sent to the poorhouse and she'd move heaven and earth to make sure Sadie and Nell didn't end up in an orphanage. She had no good memories of her own time there and some were so bad that they still haunted the worst of her dreams.

"Obliged," she said with a nod, slipping the coin into her pocket. "Got any more jobs for us?"

Conan Doyle flashed her a smile. "Well, now – perhaps I do. Do you happen to have heard of anyone with an unhealthy interest in the human ear?"

Zinnie blinked. "Sorry?"

Conan Doyle sank into his desk chair. "You know that I am a medical student at the Royal Infirmary, yes?"

Zinnie nodded.

"Something's been happening to some of the cadavers delivered for use in our learning," he said. "In the past ten days, two of them have arrived without their ears."

Zinnie shifted from one foot to the other. "Haven't you never had a corpse with bits missing before?"

"Well – yes, of course. Sometimes we get ones with a limb cut off, or some other injury. But to have two that have both lost their ears – severed cleanly, as if with a knife or some other precision instrument – that seems strange, does it not? Even to you?"

Zinnie wasn't sure what he meant by the 'even' in that question and narrowed her eyes.

Conan Doyle raised both hands in silent apology. "All I mean is that it seems obvious to me that something is amiss. Don't you agree?"

Zinnie shrugged again. "Don't seem like a very usual occurrence, no."

Conan Doyle nodded. "Yet the chief physician of the Royal Infirmary has dismissed it as a prank, perhaps by my fellow students. Why he feels they would bother with such a charade, I don't know. I've been trying to work out what might have been important enough about those men's ears that would warrant their removal."

Zinnie thought for a moment. "A punishment maybe?"

Conan Doyle grimaced. "I don't think so. As far as I can make out, the ears were removed *post mortem* – after death, not before. Not much of a punishment, eh?"

"Maybe they had something on them or in them? A tattoo? Earrings?"

"Hmm. Perhaps, but it is impossible to tell." He peered at her from his desk, as if a little surprised. "Good questions, though, Miss Zinnie. What else have you got?"

"I've got to get back…" She trailed off as Conan Doyle tipped out another half-crown into his hand and held it up.

"I'll pay for your time," he said. "I should be glad of another perspective and, forgive me for saying so, but perhaps one from the underbelly of this great city is exactly what I have been missing when it comes to 'the Mystery of the Severed Ears'. I intend to take any theories to the police, of course, especially if it seems there is risk of more, but it would be sensible to have something solid to suggest to them before I do."

Zinnie took the coin and added it to the one already in her pocket, pleased by the chink and jingle they made. A whole crown! That could feed the girls well for a week, and might even get them a night or two in a hostel on Grassmarket as well.

"What sort of men were they?" Zinnie asked. "The ones missing their ears, I mean."

Conan Doyle shook his head. "Their names are lost. They each had tattoos, however. I had it in mind that they could be sailors but, if that's the case, they could have come from anywhere, and their ship – or ships – have probably already left Leith."

"How did they die?"

"The police have concluded the deaths were accidental and are planning no further investigation. They had both suffered knocks to the head. The inspector I spoke to offered the opinion that the men were probably drunk at the time and suffered some form of misadventure." Conan Doyle shrugged. "It is possible, I suppose, but it seems an inadequate explanation to me, especially given the fact that they arrived in the morgue without their ears."

"I suppose," Zinnie said slowly, "that *when* they had

their ears cut off is significant. If it was when they died, it probably means they were murdered by whoever took their ears. If it was afterwards, maybe not."

Conan Doyle snapped his fingers. "Yes! Exactly, Miss Zinnie, exactly! I was really hoping the constabulary would investigate properly but, between you and me, I have more faith in the detective powers of a day-old trout. The police have written it off. It seems as if only I am interested in this little problem."

"Not sure what anyone can do without knowing who the men are," Zinnie pointed out. "Got to have somewhere to start."

"Then perhaps that's what you can help me with?"

Zinnie thought for a moment or two. Even if they had been dock workers or sailors, Leith wasn't her patch and getting anyone down there to talk to her would be difficult. There must be some other way.

"What about the tattoos?" she said. "Were any of them shared between the men?"

"I think so, actually, but I can't tell for sure – some had been burned off."

"Burned off?" Zinnie repeated. "What do you mean?"

Conan Doyle indicated his own chest with a swipe of his forefinger. "They both had old marks across their chests, which suggested to me that they were trying to remove the tattoos by means of scorching. They were roughly in the same place and of the same shape, though. It would make sense that the tattoos which had once been there matched."

Zinnie frowned. "Have the bodies been done away with yet?"

"No. They're still in the mortuary, awaiting dissection. Perhaps tomorrow I should go and examine them again. I could produce some sketches for you to look at."

"Good idea," Zinnie said, turning to the door with the coins jangling in her pocket. "Might give us something to go on, at least."

"Wait!" Conan Doyle snapped his fingers. "By God, why didn't I think of it before? Lady Sarah's seance!"

Zinnie blinked. "What?"

"It's tomorrow night, at Montague House on Queen Street," Conan Doyle said. "I can gather items of each man's clothing from the mortuary and ask the medium to summon their spirits. We can get the answers directly from the dead men themselves!"

"Really?" Zinnie said doubtfully. "And what do you mean 'we'?" She didn't believe in an afterlife. As far as she was concerned, there was enough trouble to deal with in this world without worrying about the next one. Yet Conan Doyle's enthusiasm seemed genuine.

"I'll need you there, Miss Zinnie, listening to whatever they say. I think the answer lies on your side of Edinburgh rather than mine. You may find significance in something I do not."

"I can't go to a seance on Queen Street!" Zinnie almost

laughed. "Your Lady Sarah would kick me out as soon as look at me!"

"She won't. When I tell her I need you there, she'll go along with it. Lady Sarah Montague is game for anything, the more daring the better. Six months ago, she was fording rivers in the Rocky Mountains in Colorado. A child from Old Town Edinburgh isn't going to scare her off." He raised his eyebrows. "You can be a maid for the evening."

Zinnie looked down at herself. She was dressed in the only clothes she owned – a threadbare pair of rough brown trousers with a grubby shirt over the top. "Will I have to wear a skirt?"

Conan Doyle grinned. "Afraid so. A clean cap too, to hide that short hair of yours. But don't worry about all that. Subterfuge will suit you, I know it already. Be at thirty-three Queen Street at six o'clock tomorrow and Lady Sarah will arrange the rest. I'll make sure of it."

Zinnie still wasn't keen. Her doubt must have shown on her face.

"I'll pay you, of course," Conan Doyle said.

"All right," said Zinnie. "Six o'clock it is."

CHAPTER 3

Zinnie made her way back towards the Old Town, the cold night wind turning her fingers and toes to ice. Above her the rain clouds had tattered into thin scraps, lit a smudged grey by the moon. A scatter of stars pricked the darkness beyond and she realized she had taken far longer with Conan Doyle than she'd intended. Sadie and Nell would be famished.

The market was dwindling by the time she got to the High Street, but she found a loaf, a chunk of drying cheese and a little milk that hadn't yet turned. The bread and cheese she shoved under one arm, then dug in her pocket for her candle stub and matches, sticking the stoppered milk bottle in there instead.

Writers' Court passageway was a pitch-black mouth as she approached. Zinnie struck a match and walked into the darkness of the narrow street, her candle casting an indistinct circle of yellow against the damp walls. Noises shivered from the tenements that reared high above her head: children crying, muffled conversations, drunken laughter. An echo rattled behind her, a stone skittering from underfoot. Zinnie glanced back towards the dim light of the Royal Mile, but she could see no one there.

On her left was the entrance to the tall tenement buildings of Writers' Court itself, but Zinnie carried on, ever deeper into the darkness, beside the wall of the Royal Exchange. Further down her candle picked out rickety steps to a broken door that stood below the level of the newer wall. The authorities had boarded up this entrance to Mary King's Close more than once, but it was always torn open again. Zinnie slipped down the steps and between the jagged slivers of wood. Beyond were more steps, leading to what might once have been a cellar for the building that used to sit above it.

Mary King's Close had once been just like Writers' Court, with tall buildings slouching towards each other either side of a narrow street. It and several other closes had all been built beside one another on the steep hill that led away from the Royal Mile. Even then, the buildings had been overcrowded and unsanitary, with families crammed in side by side. Buckets served as toilets and, when full, their contents would be flung out of the windows on to the cracked flagstones of the closes below – as well as on to any poor person who happened to be passing by at the time. The filth gathered on the ground and seeped into the lower levels, where it was dark even at noon. There was nowhere else for the people who lived there to go – Edinburgh was crowded and those that had rooms paid dearly for them, whatever state they were in. Sickness spread easily, and when the plague came to Edinburgh in the 1600s it had raged in the closes as wildly as an unchecked fire.

After that, the closes were thought to be haunted and were left to the ghosts. Eventually, the new Royal Exchange was built over the top of the abandoned streets. Below, though, the closes were still there, and so too were the lower levels of the houses, their rooms left in darkness, empty and crumbling. If one knew how to get down there, however, there was space to sleep – to live, in fact, for people like Zinnie who had nowhere else to go.

The air thickened as she descended. It was fetid with damp, with the filth of both people and vermin, growing worse and worse with each step she took. At the bottom was a room, its curved stone ceiling almost too low to stand up straight in. Her own candle was beginning to die, but there were others dotted here and there. They flickered uncertainly in the darkness, illuminating the dirty, hungry faces of the people crouched around them. In one corner an old woman was lighting a makeshift hearth on a flat stone set in the dirt floor. The smoke belched in acrid clouds, clogging the throats of those nearby, making them cough. There were no windows through which it could escape. Eventually, most of it would seep into the cracks, but the air would never properly clear.

Zinnie passed through two connected rooms like this, weaving between knots of people as she made for the spot where Sadie and Nell would be. It wasn't much, the place they called home, but Zinnie was proud of it. She'd found an old drape large enough to close off a little nook between a wall and what would have once been a fireplace. Beyond the curtain was a space just big enough for the three of them to fit.

She blew out her candle and pushed the curtain aside, clutching the girls' supper.

"Zinnie!" Nell cried, sitting up from beneath the tattered blanket Sadie had wrapped her in. "I thought you weren't coming back."

"Ach, now, don't be silly, pippin," Zinnie said, passing Sadie the milk and food before dropping to a crouch beside her sister. She ran her fingers over Nell's forehead, worried by the unnatural heat in her skin. "You know that whatever happens I'll always come back. I'm sorry. I hadn't meant to be so long."

Nell threw her arms round Zinnie and held on tight. Zinnie could feel her littlest sister trembling and felt guilty. It wasn't so long ago that Nell had been left on her own in the street like a stray when both her parents had died of sickness. She clearly had still not forgotten that fear.

"Here," Sadie said, holding out their one battered tin bowl for Nell to take. Into it she had poured some of the milk and added a hunk of the bread to soak. "Eat."

Nell let go of Zinnie and took the bowl, coughing harshly. Zinnie looked over at Sadie, who was busy tending the small fire she'd lit. They'd made a hole in the side of the fireplace by chipping away at two of the crumbling stones so that most of the smoke went up the old chimney. It probably still came out somewhere not far overhead, but at least it wasn't right in their faces. Over the flames, water was heating in their tin mug. Criss-crossing the nook above their heads was a branch that Sadie had found in Princes Street Gardens. From it hung bunches of plants, filling the place with their herbal scent as they dried. As Zinnie watched, Sadie chose a single sprig, crumbling the leaves into the water.

"There," Sadie said, setting the mug down in front of Nell. "Yarrow tea. We'll let it cool a little and then you must drink it all down – it will stop you coughing and help you sleep. Tomorrow I'll go and gather some more," she told Zinnie. "That's the last of it in my stores. I need coltsfoot too. I hadn't realized I'd run out."

Sadie's mother and grandmother had brought her from Ireland to escape poverty and starvation, but here in Edinburgh they had both died of consumption, leaving Sadie alone with the knowledge of which plants could heal and how. It had been a family tradition – all of the women in Sadie's family learned plant lore from their mothers as they grew up, and it was as natural to her as breathing. Some of the older folk in Mary King's Close muttered about Sadie. *Witch*, they called her. However, when they were desperate and sick, with no money for a doctor, they seemed to forget all about their suspicions and came to Sadie for her cures.

By the time Nell had finished her supper and drunk her tea, she was struggling to keep her eyes open. Sadie sang a quiet little lullaby as Zinnie tucked Nell in again, watching until she was sure she was asleep.

The two older girls were sharing out the last of the bread and cheese between themselves when the noise of a commotion gusted in beneath the curtain.

"Is that a fight?" Sadie asked, her face anxious. Fights in Mary King's Close were dangerous – one knocked candle and the cramped space could be alight in seconds.

Zinnie listened, frowning. "I don't think so. I—"

"A ghost!" came an indistinct cry, and then the distant sound of running feet. "A spirit! We're haunted! Haunted!"

The footsteps died away as the room beyond the curtain came alive with chatter.

"Stay here," Zinnie whispered to Sadie. She got up and slipped out into the main room, pushing her way between bodies until she reached the empty doorway that led out on to the old close. Beyond there was no sign of anything untoward. Whoever had been shouting was long gone. She turned back.

"Too much whisky," she said to her neighbours. "That's all. The only demon is in the drink."

CHAPTER 4

The next morning, Zinnie woke to the sound of Nell moving restlessly beneath her blanket, wheezing and coughing in her sleep. She fumbled for a candle and lit it, setting it in their makeshift hearth. There was no sign of Sadie. Zinnie felt Nell's forehead and found it was as hot as a furnace. She was just reaching for the bucket in which they kept their water when the curtain shifted and Sadie reappeared, worry pinching at her face.

"There you are," Zinnie said. "Where have you been?"

"I went to get yarrow but there's none left," Sadie told her, sinking to her knees on the blankets. "It's been pulled up. The coltsfoot too. I asked the park keeper and he said they were making way for new borders with prettier plants. 'No one wants to look at weeds, lassie.' That's what he said."

Nell coughed again, turning on her side in her sleep,

muttering under her breath as if she were dreaming.

"What are we going to do?" Zinnie asked. "Is there another plant you can use?"

Sadie shook her head. "Maybe there's somewhere else I can find it. The Meadows or Arthur's Seat…"

Zinnie shook her head. "It'll take too long to search on your own. And you might know what you're looking for but I don't." She put her hand in her pocket and felt the second of Arthur Conan Doyle's two half-crowns. "I'll go to Constance McQuirter. She was always talking about how she had cures for everything, wasn't she, when she lived down here? Perhaps she'll have something for Nell."

Sadie nodded. "Maybe she'll have yarrow or coltsfoot herself. Ask her first, before you let her give you anything else."

"Do you want to go?" Zinnie asked, holding out the coin. "You'd know better than anyone if she's trying to pull the wool over our eyes."

Sadie looked down at her hands. "She calls me a witch."

"Ach, that's just blather and nonsense. She wants people to go to her instead of you, that's all. Everyone knows you're better with the herbs than she is. She's just jealous and greedy."

Sadie nodded but the shadow on her face didn't lessen.

"It's all right," Zinnie said, getting to her feet. "I'll go. You look after Nell – I'll be back as soon as I can."

"Wait," Sadie said. "There's something else. The police

have put posters up. Wanted posters. Zinnie – there's a picture on them. It looks just like you!"

Zinnie dropped back to her knees. "What?"

"It's true. They're calling you a boy, but it's about us taking that watch from Bread Street."

Zinnie's stomach turned over. "But no pictures of you and Nell?"

"No, but it mentions us. It … they know what we look like."

"All right," said Zinnie, thinking. "Well, don't worry. No one in here will give us up, no matter what they think of us."

She went to leave again but Sadie caught her arm. "Be careful. We can't do without you, Zin."

Zinnie patted her hand. "Don't you worry," she said. "There'll never be a copper quick enough to catch me."

She went out, making her way through the crowded underground rooms and towards the steep steps that delivered her into a grey, wet morning. She didn't have to go far once she'd stepped back out on to Writers' Court. She crossed the narrow street and went to the door in the opposite wall, beyond which was a flight of stairs leading up. Inside, noises echoed round the cracked and crumbling walls: babies crying, drunken shouts and scuffles, an old woman's blunt, hacking cough. The air smelled of burnt porridge, old beer and worse, much worse. Zinnie made her way up, heading for the third floor.

Constance McQuirter had somehow raised enough money to move out of Mary King's Close and rent a room in this tenement instead. It wouldn't be much to most folk but to Zinnie it seemed like a palace. She couldn't imagine what it would be like to have a room of your own, a space that belonged to only you.

Zinnie found the door she was looking for and knocked loudly enough to be heard amid the rest of the Court's racket.

"Come," said a haughty voice. Zinnie rolled her eyes. Clearly, Constance thought that living in Writers' Court meant she could put on airs and graces. She pushed open the door with a grin on her face.

Constance's home was a small space that looked out over the passageway outside. The room wasn't much grander than any in Mary King's Close, despite the window. A pallet in one corner did for a bed, piled with blankets that had been smoothed out in a strange gesture of tidiness. There was a bucket of water that must have been pumped from the same well on the Mile that Zinnie and her sisters used. Zinnie's eyes were drawn to a wooden crate, which had two or three old but fine dresses draped across it. Since when did McQuirter ever have need of good clothes? Moreover, how had she been able to afford them?

Constance was standing by the window. She was a tall, thin woman with creases round her eyes and mouth and dark hair that she had twisted into a coil against the back of her head. She wore a plum-coloured dress, frayed at the edges, and had draped an old lace scarf around her shoulders.

"Zinnie!" Constance said in surprise. "I wasn't expecting you. I'm waiting for a client."

"A client?"

Constance gestured to the corner and Zinnie saw a small table on which was spread a pack of tarot cards.

"You … read fortunes now?"

Constance gave a thin smile. "Among other things. I've always had an aptitude for the spiritual."

It was the first Zinnie had heard of it. "We need medicine for Nell. She's getting sick."

"Nell… She's the newest sister, isn't she?"

Zinnie was not in the mood for Constance's games. "Can you help me or not?"

Constance tipped her head to one side and a small strand of hair uncurled itself to hang against her shoulder. "Your little Irish witchling kin doesn't have a spell to cast over her for a cure?"

"You're a fine one to call anyone a witch," Zinnie said. "You do exactly the same thing as Sadie – you just don't do it nearly as well."

Constance's eyes flashed with anger. "Watch your tongue. There's a difference between an apothecary and a witch, and if you can't tell that you're more of a fool than I thought. Dabbling like your sister does – that's witchy. What I do – that's proper doctoring."

Zinnie tried to keep calm. There was no sense in letting McQuirter rile her. "She's run out of yarrow and coltsfoot. Do you have any?"

Constance raised one hand, palm up, and waved it in a careless circle. "Do I look as if I have a garden?"

"Well then, what *do* you have?"

"It depends on what you have to offer in exchange."

Zinnie held out one of the half-crowns Conan Doyle had given her. Constance regarded the money in a way that made Zinnie's hackles rise. "It's all I've got and you know it," she said. "You'd let a bairn suffer for greed?"

Constance narrowed her eyes. "I forget you've never had a mother to beat a civil tongue into your head. No matter. I do have something for you. It's precious but I'm moved by your sister's predicament."

She went to a wooden box that stood in one corner and lifted the lid to reveal a store of bottles within. Constance took one out and handed it to Zinnie. It held a clear liquid in which a few sprigs of greenery were floating.

"What is it?" Zinnie asked.

"It's made from an ancient recipe passed down to me by my ancestors," Constance said. "It will help the girl's upset stomach."

"She doesn't have an upset stomach. She has a cough and a rising fever."

"That too," said Constance quickly, and then smiled with exaggerated patience. "It is truly a wondrous concoction."

Zinnie took it and handed over the coin in return. Constance pocketed it so quickly that Zinnie barely even saw her move.

"Now run along, there's a good girl," the woman said, turning her back. "My client will be here at any moment and I must prepare properly for the session. Readings can be so very draining for me."

Zinnie left without a word, going back down the stairs and across the narrow passageway to Mary King's Close. It was even more crowded than usual and there seemed to be an agitated sort of muttering about something going on as she passed, but Zinnie was too worried about Nell to take any notice. She pushed through their curtain to find Sadie bathing Nell's forehead with the last of their water and an old rag.

"Here," Zinnie said, thrusting the bottle that Constance had given her at Sadie, who took it and held it up.

"What is it?"

"I don't know. Some ancient family recipe she said." Zinnie took the last of the coins left over from Conan Doyle's payment out of her pocket and passed them to Sadie. "Have these too. Stay here and look after Nell. I'll go up to Princes Street on my own today. And remember, I won't be back until late – I've got to be at Montague House at six. With any luck, she'll be over the worst by the time I get home."

CHAPTER 5

After a long day of begging for coins and avoiding the policemen patrolling Princes Street, six o'clock that evening found Zinnie at 33 Queen Street. The house was five storeys high and as grand as any she had ever seen. Montague House faced the lush and leafy greenery of the gated Queen Street Gardens, a private park that was for the exclusive use of the residents of the streets that edged its land. The sun was only just beginning to set and in the last glance of the day's warmth the park's flowers were giving out great gusts of scent, wafting like perfume across the thoroughfare to where Zinnie stood on Lady Sarah's steps. It was half a mile and an entire world away from Mary King's Close.

Sadie would give her good teeth for just a few hours on the other side of those gates, she thought, as she waited for the door to open. *What sort of life would it be, to walk into a place like that whenever you felt like it?*

The butler had obviously been expecting her because, when he opened the door, he merely gave her a brisk look up and down and then let Zinnie in. She stepped through the door and stopped dead. For a moment she could do nothing but gape.

Everything in Montague House screamed expense. A glittering crystal chandelier hung above her head. Carved gold lilies wound round the banisters edging the huge staircase that led up to the first floor. In fact, there was gold everywhere, encircling mirrors and gilding the candelabra standing upon the gleaming dark wood cabinets. In places it was shot through with a piercing turquoise-blue and a deep purple, colours that shone from the heavy drapes gathered beside the windows and the fat cushions on elegant seats that looked as if no one ever sat in them. It was like being enveloped by a peacock's tail feathers.

There were curious flashes of strangeness too. The walls were peppered with carved wooden masks, feathered headdresses and pieces of huge jewellery in frames. Three curved gold daggers were displayed on a small corner table. The hat stand seemed to have spears resting in it instead of umbrellas and there was some kind of brightly coloured bird perched atop it. A second later, Zinnie was startled as the bird, which she'd assumed to be stuffed, proved to be very much alive. It gave a single unholy squawk and opened its scarlet wings, soaring up the staircase and out of sight.

"This way," said the butler, with a touch of impatience.

Zinnie followed him into another beautiful room, where the mistress of the house was waiting. Lady Sarah Montague turned out to be an extremely tall woman with a strong, smiling face and thick blond hair. She was sitting in a high-backed armchair beside the fire, but stood up as Zinnie was shown in. The dress she wore was embroidered with hundreds of tiny colourful flowers and probably cost more money than Zinnie would ever see in her life.

"Well now, you must be Zinnie," said Lady Sarah, before the butler could open his mouth. "I know absolutely nothing about you, but Arthur says he needs you to be here and so here you must be. Perkins, send up some tea, would you? And send up Dorcas too – Zinnie will need to meet her."

"Come, sit," said Lady Sarah, as the butler bowed and left.

Zinnie looked down at the grubbiness of her tattered trousers and then at the white seat of the chair Lady Sarah had indicated.

"My dear, please don't trouble yourself," said Lady Sarah, seeing her hesitate. "You should see the kinds of messes I've brought back with me to this house time and time again and it has always survived. Furniture is really quite resilient, you know, as long as you don't take a match to it. And trust me, on occasion, I've even done that when it's been necessary."

Zinnie wasn't quite sure what to say to that, and couldn't even begin to work out whether it were true, but she did as she was told and perched on the chair. Her eye was then caught by something on the floor. At first she thought it was an odd-shaped rock, but then it moved and she was shocked to see that it had a stone-coloured head and four stumpy legs. She jumped and gripped the arms of the chair.

"Oh!" said Lady Sarah, leaning down to scoop up the strange creature. It immediately retracted its head and legs so that it looked even more like a stone. "You've found Algernon! He's a tortoise. I brought him back with me from China – someone wanted to make soup out of him for me, but I wouldn't allow it. He does have an enclosure – but he prefers to roam round the house, looking for lettuce and surprising my guests. Isn't he such a peculiar, beautiful thing?"

The door behind them opened before Zinnie could think of a response and a maid came in with a silver tray loaded with a teapot and cups.

"Ah, Anne," said Lady Sarah, as the girl set the tray down. "Take Algernon, would you, and get cook to let him have some peas? He does love peas."

The maid gingerly took the tortoise in both hands and bobbed a slightly awkward curtsey before she left again.

"Now," said Lady Sarah, "I hear that Arthur needs you to be one of my maids in attendance at the seance tonight, is that right? Am I permitted to know why?"

Zinnie blinked in surprise. "He hasn't told you?"

"Not a thing. I just got a note to say you were coming and what he needs you to do."

"And you just … did it?"

"Oh, dear Arthur," said Lady Sarah fondly. "I can never refuse that boy anything. Bless him, he thinks he's going to be a doctor, but he's obviously destined to be an author. He tells the best stories of anyone I know. Whatever he's up to, I'm all for it."

"He … wants me there to listen," Zinnie said. "In case there's anything said that might mean something to me that means nothing to anyone else."

"I see," said Lady Sarah, nodding, as she began to pour the tea. "Well, actually, I don't see at all, but there you go. Perhaps it will all become clear in due course. I trust Arthur and Arthur apparently trusts you, and that's good enough for me."

"Oh yes, she's been everywhere has my lady," said Dorcas the maid later, as she showed Zinnie round the house. "Brought a bit too much of Everywhere back with her as well, if you ask me," she added, wrinkling her nose as the two girls paused to look up at another fearsome mask.

Zinnie was now in a plain black dress with a neat white pinafore over the top. Her face, ears and hands had been scrubbed with soap (quite hard – Dorcas had done the scrubbing herself) and her short hair combed back beneath a white cap. The clothes were the newest and cleanest Zinnie had ever worn, but she hated the skirt – it reminded her of her miserable days in the orphanage and it was awkward to move in. Besides, the cotton was starched stiff and scratched at her skin.

"Is there a Lord Montague?"

"Nope," said Dorcas. "There was once but he died, long time ago now, before I were ever here."

"Then who does she travel with?"

Dorcas gave her a grin. "On her own mostly. Oh, we're a fully modern household, don't you know. What are you doing here anyway?" she asked, as they made their way back down the stairs towards the kitchen.

"I'm just an extra pair of ears, that's all," Zinnie said. "One of Lady Sarah's guests wants answers from spirits that might mean more to me than him when they come."

"Oh aye? Well, you go ahead and listen. Long as you don't talk too much about what you *see*, we'll all stay friends."

"What do you mean?"

Dorcas smiled, though there was an unpleasant edge to it. "Never mind. You're smart; you'll get it. You had anything to eat today?"

Zinnie's stomach grumbled loudly in answer.

"Come on," said Dorcas. "Let's find you a bit of Cook's

chicken pie. Can't have you getting the shakes while you feed and water the great and the good, can we?"

A few minutes later, Zinnie sat amid the warm bustle of the kitchen, eating the best pie she'd ever tasted, surrounded by other servants doing the same. As she was trying to work out how she could save some of her meal for Sadie and Nell, she noticed a knot of maids and footmen in the dim light of the hallway that led to the servants' stairs. They were gathered round a figure in a hooded cloak who seemed to be passing out coins. Each of the servants took one and listened to something the figure said before giving a brief nod and slipping away. One of the maids was Dorcas.

A loud bell rang and everyone round the table at which Zinnie sat immediately stood up. The butler appeared at the other end of the kitchen.

"It's time, people," said Perkins. "Don't let Lady Sarah – or me – down this evening, will you?"

There was a general murmur of, "No, sir." Then the servants all scattered to their assigned tasks. Zinnie felt a light poke on her shoulder and turned to find Dorcas behind her.

"Come on," said the maid. "Stick with me and you'll be right."

CHAPTER 6

At dinner, the guests sat round a long table laden with food. There were large bowls of fruit that just seemed to be for show. Terrines of pressed meats were carried in, surrounded by dishes of pickles and spiced chutneys. Whole poached fish lay on silver platters and roasted game birds were accompanied by great jugs of gravy and steaming-hot vegetables. Then came the pâtés and cheeses. There was course after course of elaborate, delicious-looking food, finally topped off with sugared cakes and grapes.

"So, Lady Sarah," said one guest, over the hubbub of other conversations, "do tell of your next expedition. To the Amazon, was it you said? I'm sure I should never be so bold as to journey there myself, not even with all the protection in the world."

"Indeed, Mrs Danvers, South America is my next

destination," said Lady Sarah. "All being well, I plan to embark for Ecuador early next year. From there I shall traverse the tributaries of the great river to the jungle city of Manaus before striking out across the jungle to Rio de Janeiro. That has never been done, you know, not by a European, at any rate. I anticipate I shall be away for two years, or perhaps even more."

"Good Lord Almighty," burst out a loud voice with a broad American accent. It came from the other end of the table. All eyes turned to look at the man who had spoken. "Forgive me, Lady Sarah, but why would you even contemplate such a thing?"

Lady Sarah smiled again. "Ladies and gentlemen, for those of you who have not yet met our new acquaintance this evening, this is Mr Phineas MacDuff, of New York, New York. My dear friend Sir Walter Charles sent him to me with a letter of introduction, bidding me make him welcome among Edinburgh society."

There was a general murmur around the table. The man in question smiled indulgently and pulled a kerchief from his pocket to dab at his thin lips. Zinnie saw that the scrap of cotton had letters stitched into one corner in curling script. She wasn't surprised – MacDuff seemed like the type of man who would want to make sure people knew what he owned.

"But, to answer your question, why does anyone do anything, Mr MacDuff?" Lady Sarah went on. "To see what's out there, of course, and to experience it for oneself."

"There ain't nothing on that continent that's fit for a lady to experience, I can tell you that for nothing," said MacDuff. "Forgive my Yankee bluntness, m'lady, but you'd be better giving up the enterprise right now."

"Oh?" Lady Sarah said coolly. "Would you have said the same to Burton or Speke?"

"Of course not, but that's different."

"Is it?" The whole table had hushed. "How so?"

"Well, of course, it is in the very nature of a man to seek adventure, to desire to push beyond his own limits," said MacDuff. "But for a woman, especially one such as yourself…" He trailed off, perhaps realizing that he was entering tricky territory, especially since Lady Sarah was his hostess. "Although I suppose you will, of course, be taking a proper escort with you, comprised of former military men and whatnot."

Lady Sarah raised an eyebrow and even from across the room Zinnie could see the piercing blue of her eyes. They seemed to have become fiercer as she had listened to MacDuff's tone. Zinnie wanted her to take this loud, arrogant man to task, but when she spoke again Lady Sarah's voice was still perfectly calm.

"No. I shall attempt to find a suitable companion to take with me, but beyond that I shall be relying on local guides. Men – and women – who know the area intimately and can take me on the most efficacious routes."

This made perfect sense to Zinnie. If she ever needed to find her way in an area of Edinburgh she didn't know well, she tried to find someone who lived there to tell her where to go. After all, who would know it better? MacDuff, though, obviously thought otherwise. He'd been in the process of taking a mouthful of wine as Lady Sarah said this, and he coughed as if he had breathed in too suddenly and might choke. A strained second later, he recovered himself.

"Oh no," he said. "*Natives?* That won't do at all. You'll end up lost or, at worst, eaten. They can't be relied upon for a thing. Allow me to offer my services for your protection instead, Lady Sarah. If you want to see more of the world, I shall be embarking on a trip to the Cape late next year. You shall come with me and all will be well."

"But the Cape is not where I desire to go, Mr MacDuff. If I wanted to see a place owned by the Dutch, I should simply board a boat to Amsterdam."

Zinnie watched MacDuff shrug, as if what Lady Sarah wanted was by the by. He looked at several other of the male guests, clearly attempting to solicit their support. Zinnie felt her hackles rise. Here this man was, a guest at the generous table of Lady Sarah, who had taken him in on nothing more than the word of a friend – as she had with Zinnie herself, in fact – and MacDuff still thought he had the right to tell her what to do!

"I do believe you have been lacking a man's guidance, Lady Sarah," he suggested. "Take the advice of someone who has travelled extensively and knows—"

"Have you trekked the mountainsides of Burma, Mr MacDuff?" Lady Sarah asked, her steady voice full of an authority that cut across the man's loud bluster. The rest of the table was still quiet.

"No, m'lady."

"Have you rafted the waters of the North Platte in Colorado, in your own native land?"

"I have not."

"Have you seen the sun rise over the Blue Mountains in Australia?"

MacDuff looked away. "I've never been to Australia."

"Have you scaled the heights of Mauna Kea in the Sandwich Islands or ridden a camel on the sands of Arabia?"

The man was looking positively red-cheeked by now. Zinnie had to bite her lip to stop herself from grinning. "No, m'lady, but—"

"Then, Mr MacDuff," Lady Sarah said, with a patient smile, "I suspect I am at least as adept at travel as you are."

Still MacDuff would not be dissuaded. "I mean no disrespect, Lady Sarah, but I believe someone must speak in defence of your welfare."

Zinnie very nearly snorted a laugh at that. Only an idiot would listen to what Lady Sarah had just said and think she couldn't look after herself. Zinnie had the idea, however, that although MacDuff might have heard what his hostess had said, he hadn't really listened to her at all.

"Don't worry yourself about me, Mr MacDuff," said Lady Sarah. "I know perfectly well how to organize my own safety and travel. Not to mention my own mind."

Zinnie had absolutely no problem believing the truth in Lady Sarah's words, and wondered why MacDuff could not do the same.

"The natives will not welcome a woman travelling alone," MacDuff warned her, clearly not believing she could know better than him.

"Well," said Lady Sarah, "then I suppose I must have just been terribly lucky to date. Even so, Mr MacDuff, if there is one thing we women know how to do, it is to go where we're not wanted and yet make the journey anyway. Though in my experience such travel seems to be met with more resistance here at home than anywhere else. Is that not so, Doctor Jex-Blake?"

Zinnie expected one of the silent men around the table to answer but instead, to her utter surprise, it was a woman who replied. She was a stout, dark-haired lady in a sombre black dress with a white lace collar and a calm, strong voice.

"Indeed, Lady Sarah," she said. "Otherwise we should none of us ever get anywhere at all."

"Mr Phineas MacDuff, perhaps you were not introduced to Doctor Sophia Jex-Blake earlier," Lady Sarah went on. "Doctor Jex-Blake has just opened her practice here in Edinburgh, the first female doctor to do so in Scotland." Lady Sarah paused. Zinnie thought she caught a brief look of mischief flash through her eyes, which was just as quickly replaced by utter seriousness. "As a newcomer to these shores, Mr MacDuff, I am sure you must be looking for a skilled physician to take care of you. You should apply to Doctor Jex-Blake. She still has room to take on new clients at this moment, I believe."

There was another moment of silence as MacDuff tried to come up with a good excuse not to agree to Lady Sarah's suggestion.

"You're a long way from home yourself, Mr MacDuff," Arthur Conan Doyle said. Zinnie thought he had probably spoken just to ease the sudden and awkward silence. "What brings you to our fair city?"

"After a lifetime of my own travels, I've decided I need a home town and this great city has caught my imagination," said MacDuff, apparently relieved by the change of subject. "Over the years I have collected items of such interest that it would be selfish not to share them with others, so I've decided to open a kind of museum. It is called the House of Wonders and it will be on George Street."

That made Zinnie take a new interest in MacDuff. She knew exactly where the House of Wonders was. She had walked along George Street only the day before and noticed the large corner building with the colourful, hand-painted posters outside. Everything about it had been loud, demanding the attention of passers-by.

"Aha," said Conan Doyle. "Yes, I have passed the place

you describe. From the painted boards outside it certainly looks intriguing. Now let me see – what does it promise?" He paused with his fork in the air as he thought for a moment. "Ah yes. 'Scientific Wonders From Far and Wide, Sights Such as Those Never Before Seen on These Shores' – isn't that it?"

MacDuff smiled broadly. "Indeed, Mr Conan Doyle, indeed."

"There are also boasts about experiments in electrobiology, a reanimated rodent, the strongest woman on the continent, a living ghost and a human monkey, if I remember correctly?"

MacDuff looked pleased. "Among other things, yes. My, what a memory you have, sir."

"A human monkey?" Lady Sarah repeated, sounding entirely mystified. "What, pray, can that be?"

"You must come and see for yourself, m'lady, once the house is finished," MacDuff said. "There have been a few unavoidable delays but we are planning to stage a grand opening very soon. Sadly, as much as I adore your beautiful city, it seems as ridden by crime as any other. I have been robbed of a few valuable exhibits that must be recovered before I can invite the public inside."

"Oh, how terrible," said Lady Sarah. "I am sorry to hear that, Mr MacDuff. The police have been helpful, I hope?"

MacDuff gave an ugly snort. "I'm afraid not, m'lady. If you'll excuse me saying so, they seem rather ... uninterested."

Zinnie heard Conan Doyle chuckle and then saw MacDuff shoot him a black look that made a warning bell ring deep in her mind. Phineas MacDuff, she noted, did not like to be laughed at.

"Something funny, sir?"

"Oh no, it is only that I share your frustrations, but have found my own solution to them."

"Oh?" MacDuff watched him with interest. Zinnie still didn't like the look in his eye – there was something about him that made her skin creep as if a spider had skittered across it.

"When I need to find something lost in the underworld, it is the underworld to which I turn for help. It has never failed me so far."

MacDuff narrowed his eyes. "A good tip, sir. I thank you for it."

The door opened then. Perkins slipped in, approaching the mistress of the house and bending to speak into her ear for a moment. Lady Sarah nodded and then turned to the table.

"Ladies and gentlemen," she said, "our medium is ready for us."

CHAPTER 7

Zinnie followed the guests into a hexagonal room with a domed golden ceiling and a floor of red and black marble. The walls were entirely lined with books, volume upon volume bound in leather of greens, reds and blacks. Sconces holding great pillars of cream-coloured candles had been lit on each wall, the wax dripping to leave strange melted forms on the marble beneath. A golden chandelier hung overhead, right above a large round wooden table at which one person was already seated. It was a woman in an opulent dress with pearls glittering in her hair. Her eyes were shut.

Zinnie sucked in a shocked breath.

It was Constance McQuirter.

She stopped so suddenly that Dorcas bumped into her. Zinnie didn't know what to do. Constance McQuirter was surely no more able to speak to the dead than Zinnie herself. Lady Sarah had already taken her seat at the seance table, her head bowed in respectful silence. Conan Doyle was beside her, and Zinnie knew that he was entirely serious in his belief in what was about to happen. Otherwise why would he have paid Zinnie to be here? Which meant that Lady Sarah must also be in earnest – and she was about to be conned outright by Constance McQuirter.

Zinnie thought fast. Constance must be receiving payment – probably quite a sum too. If she was doing a lot of these evenings, it would explain how she could afford the room in Writers' Court and her new wardrobe of clothes. Zinnie went to the seance table and began to pour a glass of water for each participant. When she got to Constance, she made a show of putting the glass down a little harder than necessary.

"Please, I must have complete silence," said Constance, opening her eyes at the sound. She was putting on an accent that was vaguely French and not at all her own. "In this room, the spirits must hear nothing but my voice if we are to—" Constance broke off abruptly, staring straight at Zinnie. Zinnie glared back.

"If we are to get them to speak to us," McQuirter continued smoothly. "Please, everyone, do not open your eyes until I instruct you to do so."

Around the table, the silent party did as they were bid. Constance slipped one hand into the pocket of her voluminous skirt and drew out a gold coin, which she showed to Zinnie with a quick flash of her fingers. Glowering, she raised her eyebrows. Her meaning was clear. *Keep quiet and earn this.*

Zinnie glanced at Lady Sarah, who still had her eyes closed. She shouldn't take the money. She shouldn't let Lady Sarah be deceived. Not to mention Conan Doyle. But a whole *sovereign*! Zinnie bit her lip as Constance waited, watching her with narrowed eyes. Zinnie gave a tiny nod. Constance slipped the coin back into her pocket with an answering tip of her head.

"Very well," Constance said in her pretend sing-song voice. "Let us begin. Join hands, fair ladies and gentlemen, and open your eyes even as you open your hearts and minds. Let Madame Khartoubian see what the spirits have to offer us this night."

At least now Zinnie knew who the figure in the cloak had been and what it had been paying the servants for. Guilt warred with a little spark of excitement in her gut at being part of the subterfuge. Conan Doyle had told her she'd be good at that, hadn't he? And, now that she knew there would be no real answers from the other side for her to listen to, she could relax a little. She was about to see a show, after all.

For the next two hours Zinnie was transfixed. She had to admit that the old fraud was very good. Zinnie spent her time trying to work out how every little thing was done. The pebble and alphabet board that Constance used to 'talk' to the spirits was easy – to Zinnie it was obvious that letting the medium rest one finger on the pebble, even lightly, allowed her to move it to whatever letter the spirit 'chose'. Other 'movements of the spirits' were harder to work out. While the guests gasped as the table moved in response to a question from one of them, Zinnie wondered if Constance had a toe under one of the legs or some other way of moving it herself. When 'Madame Khartoubian' managed to reply correctly to a question asked of the loved one she was supposedly 'channelling', Zinnie had to ask herself how much time Constance had spent researching the guests she knew would be here tonight. Had she bribed others too – coachmen, stableboys, housemaids?

When the candles guttered out seemingly on cue, Zinnie wondered which of Lady Montague's silent footmen had been paid to create a draught at precisely the right moment.

Lady Sarah and her guests appeared to be entirely taken in. Conan Doyle seemed most put out that there were to be no words from the spirit realm for him, as if he had genuinely expected to be told something of use in solving 'the Mystery of the Severed Ears'. Phineas MacDuff, meanwhile, seemed desperate to receive messages from some old acquaintances of his own.

"Try again," he hissed, as Constance shook her head and professed that there was only silence. "The Kings. Are they there? Any of them?"

Constance shook her head again, the blank serenity of her face betraying nothing.

"Well, what does that mean, woman?" he demanded. "That they're not there, in the realms of the dead? Or merely that they do not wish to speak?"

"I cannot say, sir," said Constance, in her soothing French voice. "I am a conduit, not a commanding force. I can but see what the spirits want me to see."

MacDuff leaned back in his chair and crossed his arms, that black look settling once more upon his face. The seance continued, but to Zinnie it seemed that Phineas MacDuff had lost all interest.

CHAPTER 8

Later, after the seance was over and the guests had gone, Zinnie found herself downstairs with the other servants, helping to dry the dinnerware. She wondered how long it would be until she could leave, find Constance and get her coin. She hadn't seen the so-called medium since the seance had concluded, but Zinnie had no intention of letting her get away without payment. She felt bad that she had allowed Lady Sarah to be defrauded for the sake of Nell and Sadie, but her sisters, she had promised herself, would always come first.

"Zinnie," said the butler, appearing beside her. "Her ladyship wants you. I'll show you upstairs."

"Ah, Zinnie, there you are," said Lady Sarah from her seat beside the fire in the drawing room. Zinnie saw that, besides Conan Doyle, Doctor Jex-Blake was also in the room. "I must say you did a fine job tonight. I hardly remembered you weren't one of my staff at all."

"Waste of time, though," Conan Doyle said with an unhappy sigh. "Not a hint of our earless spirits. Not even a single murmur."

"Arthur's been telling us about his severed ears," Lady Sarah added. "It's most intriguing. Sophia, have you come across the like before?"

Doctor Jex-Blake shook her head. "Indeed, I have not."

"Well, I can't see that we have anywhere to try next now," Conan Doyle said gloomily. "I was sure the medium would be able to call out those spirits from among the dead."

"Perhaps they couldn't hear her," Zinnie suggested. "Without their ears, I mean."

The three adults in the room stared at her for a moment and then Lady Sarah broke out into loud, unbridled laughter.

"Oh, Arthur, I love her!" the lady declared, once she had recovered. "Zinnie, do come and work for me. You can share a room with Dorcas and train to be a housemaid here. What do you say?"

It was Zinnie's turn to stare. *Live here?* In this huge, beautiful house with all its strange decorations and key to Queen Street Gardens? With Lady Sarah, who fed her staff well and went gallivanting off round the world whenever she felt like it? There were girls out there who would consider such an opportunity as the pinnacle of their hopes, and, if things were different, Zinnie might have been one of them.

"I – thank you, my lady, that is very kind of you, really. But I can't. I've got to look after my sisters. They don't have anyone else and if I left they'd be all alone."

It was Doctor Jex-Blake who spoke up. "Your sisters? How old are they, Zinnie? You have no parents to look after you?"

Zinnie's heart turned over as she realized her mistake.

"Old enough to look after ourselves," she said shortly, the spectre of the orphanage looming over her like a malevolent ghost.

"But—"

Whatever the doctor had been about to say was drowned out by the furious ringing of the front doorbell. It was immediately followed by a ferocious knocking, as if someone were hammering against the door with their fists.

"My goodness!" exclaimed Lady Sarah, jumping to her feet. "Whoever can that be?"

They heard the sound of hurried footsteps as Perkins made for the door and opened it. As he did, there instantly came the sound of a voice, high, loud and pleading. Zinnie recognized it immediately.

"That's Sadie!"

She rushed out into the entrance hall with Lady Sarah, Conan Doyle and Doctor Jex-Blake behind her. Perkins was standing in the open doorway, blocking the entrance as he tried to talk over the unexpected visitor.

"Sadie!" Zinnie cried, wrestling the butler out of the way to see her sister, flush-faced and out of breath from running, standing on the step outside. "What is it? What's happened?"

"Oh, Zinnie," Sadie sobbed. "It's Nell! That wasn't medicine that Constance gave you. It was nothing but stale water with some old rosemary in it. The pippin's been getting worse all day – she's got a fever and I can't stop her coughing. I didn't want to leave her alone, but I had to find you. Please come home. *Please*. I don't know what to do. Everyone in the close is saying we should put her out on the street before we all get sick!"

Cold fear splashed through Zinnie. She joined Sadie on the steps, ready to run all the way home.

"Wait a moment!" came a voice from behind them. It was Doctor Jex-Blake, a look of purpose on her face. "Perkins, get my cloak and tell your man to bring my trap round. Zinnie and – Sadie, is it? Tell me where we're going."

The butler hurried away as Zinnie blinked at the doctor, so stunned by fear that she thought she had misheard.

"Zinnie!" Jex-Blake said loudly, grasping her by the shoulders. "I will come to your sister. Tell me where we need to go."

"Mary King's Close," Zinnie said hoarsely.

"*Mary King's Close?*" Conan Doyle repeated in a shocked voice, from behind them. "Surely not. I thought that place had been derelict and abandoned for years."

Zinnie shook her head, her heart thumping heavily. "One," she said. "Not the other."

Perkins reappeared, bearing the doctor's cloak as the clatter of horses' hooves sounded on the cobbles outside. He also passed Zinnie a cloth bag. Inside were her own clothes.

"Quickly," the doctor ordered. "There is no time to lose. My doctor's bag is in the trap."

"I'm coming too," said Conan Doyle, as the others made for the door.

"There's no need," said Jex-Blake.

"As capable as I know you are, Doctor, I still would not let you go there alone," Arthur said. "My mind is quite made up. Besides," he added, "I've always wanted to have a look around down there. I'm not going to miss out."

Lady Sarah followed them to the door, a worried expression on her face. "I would come too, but I shall be of no use to you and only get in the way. Goodbye, dear Zinnie – your sister will be safe in Sophia's hands, I guarantee it. Fear not."

A few minutes later, they were all seated in the trap. Doctor Jex-Blake took the reins and away they sped into the night, making for the Royal Mile.

CHAPTER 9

The bells of St Giles were striking midnight as they reached the top of Bank Street. The taverns had emptied and those people still on the streets staggered on their way through fresh rain, the worse for cheap whisky and lack of food.

They left the trap in the care of a passing boy in return for a shilling. Conan Doyle took down one of the oil lamps that hung from its rails, Doctor Jex-Blake retrieved a black bag from beneath her seat and then the two girls led the way. When they reached the broken door leading to the close, Conan Doyle hesitated.

"We're not going down there, surely?" he asked.

"Aye, we are. The closes are all under the ground now," Zinnie said, impatient. "What were you expecting, gates poured from gold?"

"Of course not. It's just I don't think—" Conan Doyle

glanced at Sophia. "Doctor Jex-Blake, I hardly feel this is an appropriate place for a lady. It's bad enough on the Mile at this time of night, but this…"

A look of irritation crossed the doctor's face. She reached out and took the lamp from him, squaring her jaw. "Oh, for goodness' sake," she said. "I didn't ask you to come, Mr Conan Doyle, and you can leave if you think you're going to impede me now. Lead on, Zinnie. I'm right behind you."

Zinnie hurried down the stairs and into the darkness below. A murmur of voices rose around her and, when she reached the bottom step, she saw that the room was even more packed than usual. There was barely any space at all between the huddles of people trying to bed down on the floor.

"My God," came Conan Doyle's low voice from behind her. "I had no idea it would be so crowded."

"There aren't usually this many people. Not all so close together anyway," Zinnie said, as she began to make her way across the room.

"It's the ghost," Sadie said. "It's all anyone's been talking about all day."

Zinnie turned to stare at her sister in confusion. "The *what*?"

"The ghost," Sadie said again. "Don't you remember – the cry we heard the other night? Well, now others are saying they've heard it. Seen it too. A *lot* of others.

They say it's haunting the lower levels. No one wants to be down there with it."

"A ghost?" Conan Doyle repeated, sounding intrigued. "And people say they've actually seen it?"

"Oh, what does that matter now?" Zinnie snapped. "Come *on*."

As she pushed her way through the room towards the corner that the girls called home, she began to fear it would be overrun. There were people crammed everywhere, making it difficult to move. But, when she reached their room, Zinnie was relieved to see that their drape was still in its usual place, once they managed to make their way through the throng.

"You'll have to wait here," she said, turning to Conan Doyle when she realized it would be impossible for them to all fit inside the girls' alcove at once. "Don't move and don't talk to anyone."

"But how can I offer protection if I'm over here?" Conan Doyle protested.

"You're the one likely to need protection in this place," Zinnie told him curtly. "Keep your eyes open. If you see trouble coming, shout as loudly as you can. All right?"

Zinnie turned away before he could argue further. Sadie was still helping Doctor Jex-Blake to pick her way across the floor. The sleepers grumbled and mumbled as they shifted out of the way to let them pass. Beyond the drape, Zinnie could hear the ugly hacking of Nell's cough.

Once she arrived by Zinnie's side, Doctor Jex-Blake didn't hesitate until she'd pushed aside the curtain. She looked down at Nell, who was asleep, breathing heavily, before turning to Zinnie.

"I don't understand," she said.

"This is Nell," Zinnie told her. "Our sister."

"But she can't be your sister," said Doctor Jex-Blake. "She's—"

"She's our sister," Zinnie said again, staring the doctor straight in the eye and daring her to say anything else.

"Her parents are both gone – dead of consumption, we think, by the sound of it," Sadie said quietly. "Zinnie found her more than a year ago, all on her own in a gutter down on Canongate. She was hungry and scared. She didn't have anyone."

"Now she has us," Zinnie said.

The doctor looked between Zinnie and Sadie for a moment, and Zinnie could tell exactly what she was thinking. Sadie's rivers of red hair and Irish accent had nothing in common with her own Scottish drawl and short pale hair, either. "So when you say that these girls are your sisters…"

"They are my sisters," Zinnie said.

Sophia Jex-Blake smiled faintly. She gave a quick nod, then put down her bag and kneeled beside Nell, pressing one hand to the little girl's forehead.

"I should have given her coltsfoot sooner," Sadie said, wringing her hands as she watched. "But at first I thought it was just a cough and I'd used all my stores. I should have found more, though. I should have—"

Zinnie reached out and squeezed Sadie's hand, wrapping her fingers round her sister's. "It's not your fault. It's not."

"You're clever to think of coltsfoot," the doctor said, glancing up at the bunches of leaves hanging over her head. "This is quite a collection you've got here. Do you know each one?"

Sadie nodded, biting her lip.

"Sadie knows every plant and how it's good for what ails a body," Zinnie said, proud despite her worry over Nell. "Everyone in the closes comes to Sadie when they're ill."

Jex-Blake didn't answer, busying herself with her bag instead. From it she pulled a strange instrument – a short pole with a shallow bowl at each end, made of white clay.

"What's that?" Zinnie asked.

"It will help me listen to your sister's heart and lungs, to see if they're working correctly," the doctor said briskly, loosening the top of Nell's grubby dress and pressing one end of the apparatus to her skinny chest. Nell moaned and coughed, trying to twist away. The doctor glanced up at Sadie. "Can you hold her still?"

Sadie kneeled on the other side of Nell and did as she was told, murmuring soft words to her sister as she held her shoulders. The doctor took a watch from her pocket and put her ear to the other end of the device.

"What—" Zinnie asked.

"Hush!" she said. "I need to listen."

Zinnie pressed her lips together. The doctor was silent for at least a minute, moving the device to a new place once or twice and staring at her watch as if she were counting seconds. Then she sat back and looked at Sadie.

"Do you want to try?"

"Oh!" Sadie looked between the doctor and Zinnie, shocked. "But I don't know – I wouldn't know what it should sound like."

"That's all right, I can tell you," said Doctor Jex-Blake, holding out the apparatus. "This is called a stethoscope. Here – try. Be quick because we must help your sister. Place it here, on her chest, and then put your ear to the cup."

As Sadie did as she was told, Jex-Blake turned to Zinnie. "Go and fetch Mr Conan Doyle. We need to get this child to a hospital as soon as possible. I can't carry her while I'm wearing this blasted skirt."

Zinnie's heart leaped and then sank in her chest. "You're taking Nell away? But—"

"Go," Doctor Jex-Blake said shortly. "If you want your sister to live, *go now*."

The doctor's words shocked Zinnie into action. She pushed her way out of the curtain and scanned the maze of bodies in the room for him. But Arthur Conan Doyle had gone.

CHAPTER 10

"Mr Conan Doyle!" Zinnie shouted over the hubbub around her. "Where are you?"

She searched the dim room, but he wasn't anywhere in the flickering candlelight. Zinnie stumbled out into the next room beyond but there was no sign of him there, either. She swore under her breath and began to push her way between those propped up against the crumbling walls.

"Have you seen a young gent pass this way?" she asked the people at her feet. "Jacket and tails, waistcoat, kerchief, definitely don't belong down here?"

Most ignored her, but there were a couple of murmurs and one raised hand, an unsteady finger, pointing.

"Thanks," Zinnie muttered. She moved through two more derelict, crowded rooms and then out of the ruined tenement building on to the narrow alley of what had, a long time ago, been Mary King's Close itself.

Once, this would have been a street with tenements either side just like Writers' Court, but now, several storeys overhead, the lower floor of the Royal Exchange had given the place an unnatural ceiling that cut out almost all light. A hundred years ago or more the crumbling buildings around Zinnie would have loomed even higher, but the upper levels of the ones closest to the Royal Mile had been cut off to create the foundations for the Exchange. They became taller and taller as the paper-thin street sloped steeply down, what was left of the old tenement walls reaching up to keep the huge building overhead level as it jutted out over one of the largest of Edinburgh's seven hills.

Further down the slope, more of the old buildings had been demolished to make way for the curve of Cockburn Street, so that now the abandoned close ended in the blank back walls of other townhouses. Between these and the rear wall of the Royal Exchange, the mouldering remains of Mary King's Close were still open to the sky. Even here the most desperate wouldn't venture into the remaining higher storeys, though, so decayed and crumbling were their wooden staircases and floors. The upper levels had rotted completely or in some cases caught fire and burned, built as they had been from wood on top of the lower levels of stone and brick. What was left were skeleton remnants of buildings that most people didn't even realize were there, and would have very little desire to visit even if they did.

Zinnie knew most of this place like the back of her hand. She'd spent hours exploring as much of the ruins as she could. There were bits of it too dingy and dangerous even for her, but to Zinnie it was home. It could never scare her. As dark as it was, as dirty as it was, it was still better than being trapped behind the walls of the orphanage.

"Mr Conan Doyle!" Zinnie yelled again, her voice echoing over the uneven flags under her feet and away down the dark slope. "Where are you?"

She began to make her way down the close, peering into the darkness of the broken buildings on either side. Usually, there would be at least a few people in all of them, but now each was empty. Zinnie couldn't understand it. There had always been talk of ghosts down here, but that hadn't stopped anyone from making use of the space before. It wasn't as if anyone had ever actually seen a ghost, after all. They'd just been afraid that they *might* see one, which wasn't the same thing at all, especially for people with nowhere else to go. They might have been afraid to be down here, but what other choice did they have?

What had changed down here, to drive these people away? Zinnie wondered. What was different now?

The darkness thickened around her as Zinnie hurried on. She passed from beneath the shadow of the Royal Exchange and into the open, looking up to see the walls vanish into a thin sliver of night far above, so clouded it was devoid of moonlight. The remnants of the buildings around her conspired with the heavy shadow of the Royal Exchange to make this place as dark as midnight. The rain was still falling, turning the hidden filth of the rough flagstones slick beneath her thin shoes. Zinnie was still wearing the maid's dress she'd been given at Montague House and had to hitch up the hem with one hand to stop it dragging in the muck.

"Mr Conan Doyle!" she shouted again, feeling her words fall dead against the walls. "ARTHUR!"

There came a sound somewhere to her left, inside one of the pitch-black rooms, followed by a muffled cry. Zinnie held out her candle and slipped through the doorway, careful to watch where she was putting her feet.

"Miss Zinnie! Here! I've dropped my light!"

Zinnie picked her way across the uneven, rubble-strewn floor to find Conan Doyle up to his knee in a hole. His foot had stepped right through a rotten board.

"Help me, please," he said. "I can't free my leg."

Zinnie set down her light and grabbed him by the arm, dragging him out. His trousers were torn and his leg was bleeding from a shallow graze.

"I told you to stay put," Zinnie said.

"I couldn't," Conan Doyle said, dabbing at the blood with a handkerchief. "This place is the stuff of legends, Miss Zinnie. And this ghost that everyone's so afraid of—"

"Ach, there is no ghost, just people with too little food and too much whisky in the gut," Zinnie said. "Come on.

Nell's got to get to a hospital, the doctor says. We need you to lift her."

Conan Doyle began to follow her out of the room, stepping gingerly over the broken floor. "Why are you so certain there's no ghost?" he asked. "It seems as if plenty of other people are convinced it's real."

"If you were going to spend eternity anywhere, would it really be down here?" Zinnie asked impatiently. "Anyway, if there's a ghost, why has it only just appeared?"

Conan Doyle shrugged as they made it back on to the close. "Maybe it's a recently deceased soul. Maybe it needs to tell someone something before it can rest. Maybe it died here." He stopped. "Aren't you at least curious?"

Zinnie turned. "No. Why are you? Why do *you* care?"

"Because this could be the proof the world needs that spirits do exist!"

"It's not a ghost."

"How do you know that?"

"Because there are no such things as ghosts."

"Then how do you explain what you saw earlier tonight? I might not have got the answers I wanted from Madame Khartoubian's seance, but other spirits convened with her, didn't they?"

Zinnie only just managed to stop herself from telling him the truth by biting her lip, hard.

"There," Conan Doyle said, a satisfied look on his face. "You can't argue with that, can you?"

"We're wasting time," Zinnie said through gritted teeth. "We've got to go. Nell needs—"

An ear-splitting shriek tore through the air, followed by the most hideous screeching that Zinnie had ever heard. It was so terrifying that she threw herself against the wall and dropped to a crouch, her arms over her head. The sound went on and on, becoming louder as if whatever was making the noise was right over their heads. Then it faded away, sucked deeper and deeper into the darkness around them. Zinnie found herself trembling, her heart beating wildly. The screaming stopped and there was a moment of absolute silence.

"If that wasn't a malevolent spirit," Conan Doyle said, sounding out of breath, "then what was it?"

Zinnie pushed herself to her feet, taking a deep, steadying breath. There was no sign of anyone or anything else except them in the street. She willed her heart to stop beating so hard. Conan Doyle was looking at her with both of his eyebrows raised, waiting for an answer, but she shook her head.

"Might have been a bird."

He made an annoyed sound in his throat. "There's no bird on this earth that could make a sound like that."

"A moggie then, trapped in a hole down here somewhere. It happens."

"That wasn't a cat!"

"I don't care!" Zinnie yelled, losing the last of her

patience. "I don't care what it is or isn't! There are more important things in this world – living things – don't you know that? And right now one of them is getting my sister to a hospital. Are you going to help or not? Because if not, I'll just leave you with your ghost and carry her out of here myself!"

Conan Doyle had the good grace to look chastened by Zinnie's outburst.

"You are right, of course," he said. "I apologize. Lead the way. Let's go and help your sister."

CHAPTER 11

"Where are we going to take her?" Conan Doyle asked, as he scooped Nell up, still wrapped in her blanket. In his arms she looked very small.

"Will the Royal Infirmary not have her?" asked Doctor Jex-Blake.

An uncomfortable look passed across the medical student's face. "I don't know. Even if they would … I don't know how long the wait would be before a doctor would see her. And I … have no real say over these things, you know."

Jex-Blake nodded. "Then we'll go to my clinic."

They made a strange procession passing through that underground world – Zinnie, her sisters and the two doctors. As they reached the steps up to Writers' Court, Zinnie thought she heard a faint echo of that terrible shriek again, far away in the darkness of the lowest levels, but she was too worried about Nell to care. She reached for Sadie's hand and the two sisters held each other fast, fingers twining together to form a bond that Zinnie promised the world would not break. She wished she could take Nell's hand too, but Conan Doyle was striding ahead.

They reached the trap and got in. Conan Doyle held Nell as the trap rattled on its way with the doctor in the driving seat. The little girl shivered and moaned as Sadie held a blanket over her, trying to protect her from the incessant rain. Zinnie ignored the cold, wet through and tired though she was. She was thinking only of Nell and how she had failed her littlest sister. Every time Nell rattled out another horrible cough, Zinnie flinched. She'd promised to keep both her sisters safe, but she hadn't been able to and now Nell was suffering for it.

The streets sped past – the long slope of Johnston Terrace, through Spitall Street to Bread Street, past the pawnbroker's where the girls had found the missing pocket watch for Conan Doyle. It was dark now, windows empty of wares like the vacant eyes of a dead body. There was the railway line into the Caledonian Railway Station, black tracks snaking under the bridge that was on Tobago Street. Zinnie had always wondered what it would be like to jump on to one of those carriages, to let the locomotive take her to somewhere strange and far away.

On, on the trap rattled, and Zinnie shivered, not just from the rain turning cold on her cheeks, but also from a sudden memory of the day she had run away from the orphanage. If there had been a convenient train then, she would have jumped on it. Instead, she had run along these very thoroughfares, desperate to get away from the orphanage, to be anywhere but the place she had been abandoned before she was old enough to walk. Halfway along Morrison Street and then left into Grove Street, and there, finally, they stopped outside a tall house bearing the number 73.

The place was dark, with no lights burning in its windows. When Zinnie ran up the steps and knocked hard on the door, there was an interval before it was opened by a sleepy-looking maid with a crooked cap on her untidy hair.

"Wilkins," Jex-Blake called from where she and Sadie were helping Conan Doyle with Nell. "Is Mrs Collins awake?"

Wide-eyed now, the maid bobbed a curtsey. "I can hear her on the stair now, Doctor."

"Good. Shout to Bill to come and take the trap. I need you to light a fire in the ward room."

Wilkins muttered a "Yes, ma'am," and disappeared, the light of her oil lamp bobbing up and down as she went.

Jex-Blake helped Conan Doyle to get Nell down from the trap, and then the rest of them followed. Inside, the building was clean, functional and uncluttered, smelling faintly of something that caught sharply at the back of Zinnie's throat.

"This way," Jex-Blake directed, and she led them along a corridor into an empty room that held four plainly made beds and a fireplace.

Conan Doyle put Nell down on one of the beds and Doctor Jex-Blake unwrapped the shivering girl from her blanket. Nell's eyes were closed and she was breathing in harsh rasps that filled the room like the sound of a saw against wet wood.

The door opened again and another woman came in, stern-looking and dressed neatly in a starched grey dress with a perfect white pinafore over it. She glanced round at the figures in the room, assessing Sadie and Zinnie with calm precision.

"Ah, Mrs Collins, there you are," said the doctor. "I'm sorry to drag you from your bed but we have an urgent case here. This is Nell. I need hot water and plenty of cloths for her."

"Yes, Doctor," said Mrs Collins. Zinnie watched her face as she regarded the little girl in the bed, but her expression didn't change. "I will see to it immediately. Is there anything else?"

"Yes," said the doctor, straightening up and indicating Sadie. "This young woman is Sadie. She is going to be in charge of making sure her sister drinks water and will otherwise assist with her treatment. Please show her where to find all she needs."

Mrs Collins hesitated for a second. "That will mean giving her access to the medical supplies, Doctor, as well

73

as the kitchens and all the spaces between the two. It will mean access to most of the house."

Doctor Jex-Blake was busy pulling Nell out of her damp clothes. "Yes."

Mrs Collins glanced at Sadie. "If you think that is wise, Doctor."

"It is," said Jex-Blake, still not sparing Mrs Collins so much as a glance. "My advice is that you give her a set of keys. It will mean you do not have to run hither and thither every time a door wants for opening."

There was another tiny pause and then Mrs Collins looked at Sadie again.

"Very well. Follow me, Miss Sadie."

It was Sadie's turn to hesitate, but only for a moment, and then she squeezed Zinnie's hand before she followed the forbidding woman from the room.

Zinnie stood, watching Jex-Blake and Conan Doyle examine her sister and feeling helpless. Every now and then, the doctor would pull something from her medical bag – the stethoscope again, to listen to Nell's heart, as well as a strip of thick black material that she wrapped round Nell's arm before holding one of her tiny wrists and looking at her watch. Nell coughed and squirmed beneath the clean sheets, waking enough to realize she was no longer in familiar surroundings.

"Zinnie!" she cried in a frightened voice.

Zinnie ran to her, pushing Conan Doyle away to

reach her sister. "I'm here," she said, grabbing Nell's hand. "I'm here, pippin – I'm always here, you know that."

Nell struggled up until she was sitting and threw her arms round Zinnie's neck. Zinnie hugged her, feeling how hot she was, and then pushed her gently back down.

"Where am I?" Nell asked groggily, looking around with feverish eyes. "I want to go home. Take me home!"

"I can't, pippin," Zinnie said, stroking Nell's hair and holding on to her hand. "You're not well but you'll be better soon. Then you can come home. I promise. Hush now. Let the doctors make you well."

Nell's eyes fluttered shut again and Zinnie leaned back, just in time to catch a glance between Doctor Jex-Blake and Arthur Conan Doyle that made her stomach drop to her knees.

CHAPTER 12

"What is it?" Zinnie asked. "Tell me. She's here now. You can look after her. You're a doctor. You can make her well. Can't you?"

Doctor Jex-Blake and Conan Doyle shared another look.

"Don't do that!" Zinnie hissed, curling her fists in anger. "I hate it when people do that, as if you think we can't see you, or are too stupid to notice! Just *tell* me!" Her heart was thumping fast, and she was afraid.

"Zinnie," said Doctor Jex-Blake gently, as she drew her to the other side of the room. "We will do all we can, of course we will. But you must understand – if it is consumption, there will be no cure."

Zinnie felt her eyes fill with stinging tears and she dashed them away with an angry hand. "You mean she'll die."

The doctor glanced at the little figure in the bed,

her face troubled. "We will do everything we can to prevent that. I promise you, Zinnie. But, if it's not tuberculosis, it's bronchitis, and that is almost as dangerous – although, at least with bronchitis there is hope. Do you understand?" Doctor Jex-Blake laid a hand on her shoulder and squeezed gently. "As I said, we will do everything we can. She needs rest, clean air and we must try to clear the mucus from her lungs."

At that moment Sadie came back into the room with Mrs Collins at her shoulder. Sadie carried a large bowl of steaming-hot water, while the matron's arms were laden with white towels.

"Now I must tend to your sister," the doctor said quietly. "You are welcome to stay, Zinnie, but—"

"No," Zinnie said, feeling useless and hating it. "There's something I have to do. I'm going to go. I'll be back later."

Sadie looked at her, worried. "You're going to find Constance, aren't you?"

Zinnie didn't answer – she knew she didn't really need to. No one crossed Zinnie or her sisters the way Constance McQuirter had. No one.

Conan Doyle left with her, his face grey and lined with tiredness.

"Thank you," Zinnie said. "For what you did for Nell. For trying to help. I'm sorry I got vexed."

He smiled slightly. "I quite understand. I have a tendency to get carried away with theories and what-ifs instead of concentrating on what's in front of me."

Zinnie blinked, remembering what Lady Sarah had said about him being better suited to a different occupation. "Not sure that's the best way for a doctor to be," she observed.

Conan Doyle looked at her for a second, shocked by her bluntness, and then laughed outright. "You are probably right, Miss Zinnie. But doctoring is what I'm training for and at this moment I should be preparing to attend a lecture about the workings of the cardiovascular system." He gave her a brief bow and they parted ways.

Zinnie hurried back towards the Mile. A weak sun was just beginning to rise above the rain-washed horizon as she reached the mouth of Writers' Court. Before she could turn into it, though, something caught her eye further down the Mile – a figure she knew well, standing with another she also recognized, though not as readily.

It was Bartholomew Talbot. He was speaking to the blustering American, Phineas MacDuff.

Zinnie backed into the dawn shadows, frowning as she watched the pair talk quietly together, heads bent in what looked like conspiracy. Talbot nodded at something MacDuff said and then each man withdrew. MacDuff touched the brim of his hat in farewell and Talbot jerked his chin in answer. Then MacDuff left, marching away down the Royal Mile towards Cockburn Street, swinging the heavy walking stick he carried. A second later, Zinnie realized that Talbot was coming her way, heading directly for Writers' Court. She fled down the passageway and into the tenement entrance, ducking into the darkness behind the door.

There came a harsh whistle, which she recognized as Talbot's, and a moment later his footsteps were joined by four more sets – his men, coming to do his bidding.

"Look sharp, gents," Talbot said, as the group passed the doorway inside which Zinnie hid. "We've got a job to do and it'll pay well if we get it right."

They moved on into the lessening darkness, heading for Mary King's Close. Zinnie strained to hear anything more, but could make out nothing of use. She stood still for a second, pondering. She remembered what MacDuff had said at Lady Sarah's dinner table. It would seem that he'd taken Conan Doyle's advice and found someone in 'the underworld' to help him recover his pilfered exhibits.

Talbot's a bad choice, she thought to herself. *He'll likely keep whatever it is for himself if he does find it or else aim to sell it back to MacDuff for a far higher price.*

Still, that wasn't her problem. It wasn't as if she were inclined to do MacDuff any favours herself. Zinnie remembered the black look that had passed through his eyes when he'd thought Conan Doyle was laughing at him, his anger when Constance had not been able to give him what he wanted at the seance. Zinnie had survived on these streets by listening to her gut, and there was something about the American she really didn't like.

Pushing both MacDuff and Talbot from her mind, Zinnie made her way up into Writers' Court. The stairs here were crowded, figures folded uncomfortably against the walls as they tried to slumber.

"What's going on?" Zinnie asked one old man, whose tired face was lined with more wrinkles than a wizened apple. "Where have you all come from?"

He shifted and squinted up at her with rheumy eyes. "The closes. Can't stay down there no more. Not with that spirit abroad. Vicious, she is. Evil."

"You'd rather sleep here?" Zinnie said with disbelief. "Just because you've heard tell of a ghost?"

"Ain't just *heard* about it," the old man said. "Seen it with my own eyes and heard it with my own ears. Never going back down there now. Not for the wide world and all that's in it."

Zinnie shook her head. "That's daft. It's just a story. That's all. A story!"

"Only one as hasn't seen it would say so," the old man said, his jaw setting in a stubborn line.

"Aye," said a woman beside him, waking from a fitful sleep. "'Tis true. I seen it too. So have we all here. It's real, right enough. Real and evil."

More murmurs of assent rippled round the mouldering stairwell. Zinnie shook her head and pushed on upwards, wading through people until she reached Constance's door and banged on it with an unforgiving fist. When it opened a crack, she pushed against it, hard, forcing her way into Constance's room before the trickster could shut it in her face.

Constance regarded Zinnie with narrowed eyes. "Ah, so it's you. Come for your gold coin, I suppose."

"Among other things," Zinnie hissed. "You sold me a bottle of old water as medicine for my sick sister. I want what I gave you for it back and the same again besides. *And* I want my sovereign."

Constance's lip curled. "Think to rob me, do you? You'll not get away with that, you little flotsam wretch."

"What I'm asking isn't robbery," Zinnie said in a low, dangerous voice. "But you know what is? Taking money off rich folks and pretending to conjure the dead as a medium."

A shadow passed over Constance's face. She turned away and Zinnie knew she had the woman beat. All it would take was Zinnie to tell Lady Sarah or Conan Doyle the truth about 'Madame Khartoubian' and Constance would be back in Mary King's Court with all the other destitute of Old Edinburgh in no time, or worse, locked up for good. After all, Zinnie had seen the workings of her tricks first-hand, and it wouldn't take much to get the likes of Dorcas to spill the beans and back Zinnie up, not if the alternative was the servants ending up in jail for helping to defraud their mistress.

"What were you doing there last night anyway?" Constance asked. "How does a street rat like you end up in Montague House?"

81

"If I were you, I'd be more concerned about my own skin than other people's," Zinnie told her. "Give me my money, Constance, and be grateful I'm not asking for more."

There was another pause. Then Constance went to the clothes laid out on one of her crates and dug beneath them until she pulled out a small drawstring pouch. From it she took a sovereign and a crown and held the coins out. Zinnie opened her hand for Constance to drop them into her palm. She hesitated for a minute, then let go of the money. Zinnie closed her fist round it.

"Don't be thinking this is the end, McQuirter," she said. "I've a long memory and a very short temper, especially when it comes to people who cross me. You still owe me. You will for a long, *long* time."

CHAPTER 13

Zinnie kept her fingers wound tightly round the coins in her pocket as she left Writers' Court and went to buy the first fresh loaf of bread and bottle of milk she'd had in months. She'd never had so much money before, and between her lack of food and sleep, and the feeling of the coins in her hands, Zinnie was light-headed. She would save every penny she had left, Zinnie decided, and when Nell was better – because she *would* get better – they would stay in one of the hostels on Grassmarket for a whole week and eat at least one hot meal every day. Surely that would be enough to make the littlest of them strong again?

This thought buoyed Zinnie up as she went home, although she was so tired that she didn't even light a fire in the grate. Instead, she ate a bit of the bread and drank some of the milk she'd bought, changed back into her old trousers and shirt and then huddled up in the blankets, all the while missing her sisters. Zinnie fell asleep almost straight away but kept being woken up by noises from outside the curtain. The room beyond was so crowded that no one could move without jostling someone else.

Still, she slumbered fitfully, dreaming in fragments of worry and fret. She saw Nell's fevered, tearful face looking down at her from a high window she couldn't hope to reach. She saw Sadie, starvation-thin, standing on a bare black crag beneath a sky full of snow, shivering and alone. She saw Lady Sarah holding a curved sword as big as her arm as she hacked her way through a jungle of gigantic leaves, oblivious to a gleaming jewel-green snake that was winding itself round her neck, jaws open, fangs dripping venom as it readied to strike. She saw Conan Doyle, knee-deep in severed ears, shouting at her that she had failed him. Shouting, he was, shouting, *shouting*—

Zinnie jolted awake with a start and realized that the shouting was real. It was coming from the room beyond the curtain, along with the heavy sounds of a brawl. She scrambled up and threw back the drape to see two men grappling with each other, onlookers trying to get out of the way. A candle stood on the floor near their scuffling feet, the flame stretching and guttering every time they came close.

"Stop!" Zinnie shouted. "This is stupid! If you knock a candle over…"

Neither the men embroiled in the fight nor the onlookers took any notice of her.

Zinnie felt a pit of despair open up in her chest. Living in Mary King's Close had been hard even before this so-called ghost arrived, but now – now it was unbearable. Everyone was packed in so close together and they were all so on edge that it was like living in a powder keg. Sooner or later, something terrible would happen.

I can't let Sadie and Nell come back to this, Zinnie thought hopelessly, watching the men try to tear each other apart, and over what? A patch of filth no one in their right mind would want. But where else could any of them go? Zinnie's new-found wealth was temporary and there was nowhere else, not for the likes of them, not unless they went to the poorhouse. Nell was more likely to end up in an orphanage. If that happened, the sisters wouldn't be together any more and Zinnie wouldn't be able to look after them. And she'd promised Nell she'd always be with her – there was no way she was going to break that promise. Especially not because of some ridiculous ghost that didn't even exist.

I have to go down there, she thought. *I have to find whatever's causing all this fuss. If I can stop the noises – free whatever it is making them – then eventually people will start to spread out again.*

Decision made, Zinnie reached out and plucked one of the candles from the wall.

"Oi," said a woman crouched below it. "What do you

think you're doing, you thieving wretch?"

"I'm going to get rid of the ghost," Zinnie told her. "Once and for all."

The woman made a rasping sound in her throat that Zinnie belatedly realized was supposed to be laughter. "Oh aye," she croaked. "Scrawny street rat against an evil spirit from the beyond. You'll be eaten alive, girl."

Zinnie ignored her, pushing her way towards Mary King's Close and out on to the narrow passageway. She could hear the noise of those crammed in behind her, but the close itself was deserted. There were no echoes of footsteps stirring on the uneven flags that sloped away from her, no whispers or shouts or laughter, no sounds of fighting. It was the quietest Zinnie had ever known it. She shivered slightly. The abandoned street was creepy, no doubt about that, with its crumbling skeleton buildings, towering shadows and strange roof overhead. The sun had risen higher in the sky now, but barely any light filtered down to her, even once she'd stepped out from beneath the overhang of the Royal Exchange.

Zinnie pulled her knife out of her pocket with her free hand and flicked it open, steeling herself. Then she began to walk down the steep hill. Overhead it was raining again. She followed a rivulet of water as it trickled along by her feet, catching the light of her candle like a ribbon of pure gold in the gloom. She kept expecting someone to come the other way or to appear out of one of the rooms on either side of her, but all was quiet, until her toes struck a loose piece of brick. It skittered away from her foot, bouncing and rolling, the sound echoing off the walls and into the deeper darkness beyond.

A shriek started up somewhere in the maze of deserted rooms ahead of her, that awful demon screech that was driving everyone down here to madness. It tore at Zinnie's ears and rattled her insides. She dropped to a crouch, looking up into the mizzling rain, half expecting to see a hideous spectre coming for her. But there was nothing above her but ruin and the faint swell of dim afternoon light.

Zinnie got up, willing her heartbeat to return to normal as the shriek faded. She wished Sadie were with her – having her sister by her side always helped her to be courageous. Zinnie swallowed hard and forced herself to carry on. Candle in one hand, knife held out in the other, she reached the bottom of the slope. Whatever the sound was, it had come from the mass of rooms that stretched out in a tangle to her left. She stood beside the gaping dark of an empty doorway, trying to peer into the black. The yellow flicker of her light barely penetrated beyond the first two or three feet of broken floor.

Another volley of frantic demon shrieks echoed towards her off the walls, followed by a faint sound that she could barely make out. Zinnie's blood was pounding in her ears but she strained to listen, to hear around the bright noise of the screams. Was it ... *footsteps*?

She gritted her teeth against her fear and ploughed into the room, holding the candle low to light her way round any holes in the floor. This part of the close was the most dangerous – there were many places into which a person could fall and never find their way out, even if they survived the drop. Ahead of her, more shrieks burst through the darkness.

Zinnie forged on, stepping over rubbish and filth, climbing between fallen rafters and piles of crumbling brick. The screams stayed ahead of her until they didn't. Suddenly they were above her. Zinnie raised the candle, knowing what she would see. The ceiling of the room she was in had collapsed completely, as had the one above that, so that she was standing in a void that stretched up and up, the last remaining broken planks and beams of the disintegrated floors jutting out from the tattered walls.

The shrieking came again. Zinnie searched the darkness but saw nothing. From her previous explorations of this room, she knew she could go no further. The floor had collapsed, just like the ceiling above – if she went any further, she would step straight into a gaping hole, below which was nothing at all but thin air and death. She lowered her candle and checked her footing. She'd tried several times before to find a way round the void to the rooms beyond, but she'd never been able to get across. To her right was a wide spur of floorboards that still stood firm, but they too had crumbled into nothing before reaching the other end of the room.

Another shriek, this time so close it felt as if the thing making it were right beside her. Zinnie gasped and dropped the candle. It rolled amid the debris and went out.

Silence.

Then there it was. A ghost. A *real* ghost.

Zinnie's breath froze in her lungs.

The spectre floated just an inch or so off where the floor should be, in a patch of darkness no human could reach. It was shrouded in a cloak with a heavy hood, but the figure lifted its arms and the hood fell back a little. Zinnie saw part of a white face, the mouth working into the shape of a scream as that horrible shriek came again.

The apparition glowed. Zinnie stared at it across the hole in the floor, afraid but fascinated at the same time. Had Conan Doyle been right, after all?

The shriek came again, a sound so cold and inhuman that it curdled Zinnie's blood. Then the apparition vanished, the scream dying as if it had been sliced in half with a knife. Everything was silence and darkness. Zinnie snatched up her fallen candle, but was shaking too hard to light it. She held her breath, afraid to make a sound in case doing so told the spirit where she was.

CHAPTER 14

It felt like an age that Zinnie crouched there in the dark, growing stiff with cold. She was just beginning to think that it might be safe to move when she heard a new sound. It was little more than a whisper, the voice hoarse and rough.

"Ruby," it said. "Ruby, Ruby."

There was an answer, not in words but in little chittering noises, and then the sound of too many feet. The hairs on the back of Zinnie's neck stood up as something pattered down the wall, dislodging dust and fragments of loose brick and stone that showered down from above.

"Safe now," said the grating voice after a moment. "Gone."

There came more sounds, the noise of shuffling and then a match being lit. Zinnie saw a light bloom in the darkness, a tiny flower of yellow flame. What it illuminated was the outline of a small figure in a dark cloak. Zinnie gripped her knife and readied herself as the figure began to edge its way round the hole in the floor, coming in her direction. Zinnie couldn't understand quite how whoever it was could manage to find their way, but nonetheless the figure kept coming, slowly but surely. She waited until it was within touching distance and then she stood up, striking her own match and lighting her candle.

"So," she said, as the light flared around her. "I was right after all – not a spirit!"

The figure jumped in fright, knocking back the cloak's hood to reveal a mop of dark hair above a pale round face with hooded eyes, a snub nose and a mouth open in a gasp of fear. Before Zinnie could move again, something flew at her, a snarling, screeching ball of fur that launched itself straight at her face. Zinnie cried out as sharp claws scratched her cheeks. She put her hands up to defend herself, still clutching the knife. There was a little animal cry of pain and the thing fell to the ground, whimpering.

"Ruby!" cried the figure in the cloak. It threw itself to the ground beside the bleeding creature.

Zinnie stared at the bundle of fur, at the 'demon' whose cries had so terrified Mary King's Close.

"A *monkey*?"

The figure in the cloak was beside itself, picking up the little black-and-white creature and cradling it as it bled. The animal was whimpering, sounding for all the world as if it were crying, hiding its face in its owner's cloak.

All at once, Zinnie's fear was replaced by pity. She crouched down.

"I'm sorry," she said. "I didn't mean to hurt it. Let me see – maybe I can..." She reached out but the hooded figure cringed back. "I just want to help," Zinnie promised. "Please let me."

Reluctantly, the figure opened its arms a little, although the monkey just tried to burrow deeper into them. The fact that it was moving and its eyes were still open told Zinnie that it probably wasn't in danger of bleeding to death, at least not straight away. She shuffled closer and traced the source of the blood to one of its spindly little arms. There was a narrow cut just below the creature's left shoulder, but thankfully it wasn't too deep.

"Well," Zinnie said, relieved, "I think it looks worse than it is. It will heal if we wrap it up. Do you have anything that we could use? I don't."

The face that looked up at Zinnie was streaked with tears and she saw that it was a girl, probably about the same age as Sadie, although much smaller. There was something different about her, and for a moment Zinnie studied her face. Then the girl sniffed and wiped at her eyes with one hand.

"My cloak," she said, in that low, rough voice. "Tear it."

She didn't let go of the monkey, so Zinnie nodded and grasped the edge of the wool garment. "I'll try not to use too much."

"Don't matter," the girl muttered, her attention back on her pet.

Zinnie used her knife to nick the fabric of the cloak and then tore off a narrow strip. She put the knife back in her pocket and reached for the monkey's arm, but it screamed and squirmed deeper into the girl's arms.

"Ruby," the girl said in a whisper. "Be good. Be good."

The little monkey stopped moving, blinking up at her mistress. The creature still flinched as Zinnie bandaged its hurt arm, though, keening as she tied a knot over the wound.

"Ruby?" Zinnie asked quietly. "That's your monkey's name?"

The girl nodded, sniffing.

"What about *your* name?" Zinnie asked. "I'm Zinnie. What are you called?"

The girl cringed away, her eyes darting from side to side as if looking for a way to escape.

"Don't run," Zinnie said, holding up her hands in a placating gesture. "I want to help you, I promise. And I think you probably need help. Or at least a friend?"

The girl's eyes met Zinnie's with a little frown. "Aelfine," she said.

"Aelfine? That's your name? It's pretty."

Aelfine looked down at the monkey again. "That's what ma called me. Everyone else calls me –" her face crumpled – "the Human Monkey."

"That's horrible," Zinnie said, wondering who on earth would call a person something so awful. She shifted on her haunches. Her legs were going to sleep and the damp cold of the abandoned room was seeping into her bones. "What do you like to be called?"

Aelfine looked up with another frown, as if this wasn't something she'd ever had to think about before. It took her a moment to answer. "Aelfine."

"OK then," Zinnie said. "Aelfine it is. Why don't you and Ruby come with me and you can tell me what you're doing down here and why you've been scaring folks to death."

Fear skittered across Aelfine's face. "Don't want to go back," she said. "Can't go back."

"I'm not going to make you go anywhere," Zinnie promised. "But it's cold here and it's not a good place to sleep. If you come back with me, you can stay with me and my sisters. It's warmer than here."

Aelfine blinked up at Zinnie. "Ruby can come too?"

Zinnie smiled. "Yes, Ruby can come too."

Aelfine smiled back and the expression lit up her face as if the sun had suddenly risen in the middle of the darkest part of Mary King's Close.

"Come on then," Zinnie said. "Best hide Ruby under your cloak, though, eh?"

CHAPTER 15

By the time they got back to the room, the fight had ended. Zinnie led the little cloaked figure towards their corner. Something – a vague memory – kept nudging at her mind, but when she tried to chase the thread it vanished. It was something Aelfine had said, something that was ringing a vague but insistent bell that wouldn't be silenced.

Zinnie pushed back the drape to find Sadie, a worried look on her face.

"Zinnie!"

"Sadie," Zinnie said, as the two sisters hugged. "What are you doing here? Why aren't you with Nell?"

"She fell asleep but I couldn't. I wanted to see if you were all right. I'll go back before morning—" Sadie broke off as she noticed Aelfine, partially hidden by her cloak, standing behind her sister. "Who's this?" she asked, surprised.

Zinnie ushered Aelfine into the small space and pulled the drape firmly shut behind them.

"This," Zinnie whispered, "is the ghost of Mary King's Close."

"Whatever do you mean?" Sadie asked in astonishment.

"Aelfine's the one who's been scaring all and sundry down there," Zinnie said, still in a whisper.

"What?" Sadie said, still confused. "But why?"

"I don't know yet," Zinnie admitted. "But she obviously needs help."

Aelfine hadn't moved at all since she'd stepped through the curtain. She stood there, motionless and mute. Sadie looked at Zinnie with a perplexed expression. Zinnie made a face and shrugged.

"It's all right, Aelfine," Zinnie reassured her quietly. "You can take your cloak off now. Sadie will be your friend too. She's my sister."

Aelfine just pulled her cloak more firmly around herself and ducked her head. There came a slightly muffled chattering from beneath the heavy material. Sadie's eyes widened and she stared at Zinnie.

"Ah yes," Zinnie added. "There's Ruby too."

"Ruby?"

"Aelfine's pet monkey."

"A *monkey*?" Sadie exclaimed.

"Shh!" Zinnie said hurriedly, grabbing her arm and listening to see if anyone outside had taken notice of her sister's shocked squeak. There was no sign that they had.

"How on earth has she got a *monkey*? Who *is* she?" Sadie whispered.

"I don't know that yet, either," Zinnie said. "But she's – *they* are cold, hungry and scared, and they're on their own. You remember what that's like, don't you? We've both been there, haven't we? So they need help. All right?"

Sadie hesitated for a moment, still looking unsure. But then, to Zinnie's relief, she nodded.

"Come on, Aelfine," Zinnie said. "Sit down. Sadie will light the fire and make you some hot milk. Won't you?"

"Of course I will," Sadie said, stirring herself and moving over so that there was room for all three of them to sit on the threadbare blankets.

Aelfine moved slowly, sinking to her knees, though she still didn't take off her hood. Sadie lit the fire and Zinnie poured some of the milk into the tin mug and handed it to her. For a while they listened to the crackle of the fire and the faint burble of voices from outside. Then Sadie took the milk from the flames, put a hunk of bread into it and held it out to Aelfine.

"It's hot," she said. "Be careful."

Aelfine pushed her hood back just enough to see what she was doing, revealing her pale face. Sadie looked at Zinnie with another frown.

"Thank you," Aelfine whispered. "Can Ruby have some bread?"

Zinnie smiled and tore off another chunk of bread to pass to Aelfine. "Course she can. Here."

Beside her, Sadie jumped as Ruby's little black-and-white head appeared from beneath the cloak. The monkey chattered as she grabbed the bread and began to stuff it into her mouth.

"Say thank you," Aelfine whispered. Ruby stopped eating and chattered again as she looked between Zinnie and Sadie, seeming for all the world as if she were actually thanking them for her food.

"A monkey," Sadie said faintly, as she gazed at the animal in wonderment. "Here, in Mary King's Close! I never thought I'd see such a thing with my own eyes."

Zinnie watched their two little guests eat, still trying to work out what was niggling at her. "Where did she come from, Aelfine?" she asked quietly. "Ruby, I mean."

Aelfine froze and seemed suddenly furtive, her eyes darting from side to side as she avoided looking at Zinnie. "Far away," she mumbled. "From another country."

"I know that," Zinnie pressed. "But how did *you* get her?"

For a second Zinnie thought the girl's face was going to crumple into tears. Ruby sensed the change in her mistress immediately and dropped her piece of bread, wrapping her arms round Aelfine's neck and chattering into her ear.

"I didn't steal her," Aelfine said, her voice fracturing. "Mine. Always been mine. Where I go, Ruby goes. Like ... sisters."

Sadie reached out and gave Aelfine's arm a gentle squeeze. "Well, we know what that's like, for sure," she said with a smile, as she glanced at Zinnie. "Sisters are so important, aren't they?"

Aelfine nodded, tears in her eyes.

"It's all right," Zinnie said, in a soothing voice. "I don't think you stole her. I'm just trying to work out where you both came from, that's all."

Aelfine stared into her mug, Ruby still pressing against her cheek. Then, in a mumble that was barely there at all and as if it explained everything, "*He* calls me the Human Monkey."

"I've heard that before," Zinnie said, realizing what had been tickling her memory ever since the first time Aelfine had said it. "I heard it at Lady Sarah's." She snapped her fingers as the answer finally presented itself. "Phineas MacDuff! Conan Doyle said that one of his posters for the House of Wonders talked about a 'human monkey'! Is that where you came from, Aelfine? Did you get lost? We can take you home if—"

Aelfine emitted a wail and burst into tears, dropping her now mostly empty mug on the dirt floor and curling up into a ball with her arms over her head. "No!" she cried.

"Aelfine!" Sadie exclaimed, putting one arm round the girl and squeezing gently. "It's all right!"

Aelfine went on sobbing. "I'll be good. I promise! Ruby and I will be good, we'll be good…" As her words dissolved into sobs, the monkey wrapped her arms round her mistress, looking at Zinnie with obvious reproach.

Zinnie and Sadie stared at each other in alarm. "I'm not going to make you go anywhere," Zinnie promised, over the sound of Aelfine's distress, as Sadie rocked with her. "We just want to help you, in any way we can."

Aelfine, though, would not be comforted. She cried and cried, opening her arms only so Ruby could crawl into them and hug her tightly. Sadie let her go, leaving her to Ruby. Aelfine sobbed until the exhaustion of it all crept up on her and she curled up with her knees to her chest, Ruby still in her arms. Zinnie and Sadie watched as the girl's sobs slowly trailed off into a restless slumber.

When it was clear she was definitely asleep, Sadie pulled a blanket over the awkward figure. Then she looked at Zinnie, worry written all over her face.

"The House of Wonders?" Sadie asked in a whisper. "What's that?"

"It's that new place of amusements that's opening on George Street. Don't you remember? We saw it the other day."

"Oh yes," Sadie said. "But how can she be from there?"

Zinnie shrugged. "I don't know. It was the talk at Lady Sarah's. The owner was there – Phineas MacDuff."

Sadie looked at Aelfine's sleeping face with a slight frown. "There's something … different about her, isn't there? Her face … her voice … as if her tongue's too big for her mouth. Is she sick?"

"I don't think so," Zinnie said. "She doesn't *seem* sick."

"If she is…" Sadie trailed off uncertainly.

"You could take her with you to Doctor Jex-Blake's," Zinnie suggested. "But I don't think she is. I think it's just how she is."

Sadie nodded. "What do you think she means when she says she's 'the Human Monkey'?"

"I don't know," Zinnie said grimly. "But it doesn't sound like anything good, does it?"

"You're going to find out, aren't you?" Sadie asked, turning to look at her.

"Of course I am." Zinnie said.

CHAPTER 16

The House of Wonders was situated in a tall building at the corner where Hanover Street crossed George Street. Early morning found Zinnie staring up at the large billboards that had been erected either side of the huge double doors. They were full of elaborately painted words picked out in black and red, with little pictures dotted here and there in-between. Zinnie couldn't read most of what they said. The orphanage had tried to teach her, but she had never found it possible to turn letters into words that made sense. It was one of the reasons they had beat her, calling her lazy and stupid, locking her in a room with a slate and chalk for hours without food and water as if that would somehow make her learn her letters.

Zinnie tried the front doors, but as she expected they were locked. It was probably for the best – she wouldn't have wanted to announce herself by walking in so obviously anyway. She went back down the short flight of steps and looked for a rear entrance instead. There was a narrow alley that led away between the House of Wonders and the building next door. Zinnie slipped down it, glancing behind her to check that no one was watching.

The alley sloped up a little and then joined another that was wide enough for a cart to pass through. It cut behind not just the rear of the House of Wonders but all the other buildings on the street. Here were the delivery entrances, so that the common tradespeople need not be seen hefting goods through the front doors. After all, it wouldn't do to spoil the view for the gentry.

Zinnie slipped in amid the mass of folk carrying wares this way and that. Ahead, set in what must be the rear of MacDuff's establishment, she could see another pair of double doors. These were far rougher than the grandly polished wooden ones that marked the entrance to the House of Wonders. Their red paint was faded and peeling and the flags on to which they opened were cracked. But there was a cart stopped beside them as a series of figures in work clothes hurried to and fro, carrying wooden crates of varying sizes into the house.

Zinnie pulled her cap down more firmly on her head and went closer, approaching the cart with quick confidence, as if she were part of the work crew. She kept her cap low as she reached up towards the cart so that the man standing on it could pass her something to carry. A moment later, she found herself in possession of a heavy crate made of rough wood that would have splintered into her palms had the skin of her hands not already been roughened by her life on the streets.

She gritted her teeth and turned towards the doors as she struggled not to drop the heavy box.

"Oi!" said a voice from the cart.

Zinnie paused, heart beating hard. Had he spotted that she wasn't supposed to be there? She kept her head down as she turned slightly, ready to drop the crate and make a run for it if she had to.

"I'd be careful with that if I were you, boy," the man said. "He makes us pay double the worth for breakages and it'll be coming straight out o' your wages if you drop whatever fancy tat's inside. All right?"

Zinnie nodded and turned away, heart thumping. She moved as fast as she could, joining the stream of workmen carrying their own loads.

By the time she got inside, Zinnie's muscles were burning with the effort of holding the crate. The place was even busier within, crowded with workmen of all sorts hurrying here and there. The sound of banging and hammering filtered down a narrow flight of stairs, while on the lower level, where Zinnie was, shouted directions and the noise of crates being ripped open emanated from large, echoing rooms.

"Get a move on, will yer?" said an irate voice behind her.

Zinnie stumbled forwards and just managed to set down the crate before she dropped it completely. Around her were piles of similar boxes, some far larger and some much smaller than the one she'd carried. They were stacked everywhere. In one corner a man in a finer suit of clothes than any other in the room was busy prising off the tops, issuing orders about what to do with the contents to a younger, nervous-looking man who kept nodding and jotting things down on a sheaf of paper.

Zinnie looked around but everyone was too intent on their own tasks to take any notice of her. She slipped out of the room as if she were heading back to the laden cart, but instead she made for the stairs that curved out of sight as they led to the upper floors. She ran up them, stomach clenching as she listened for a shout that would tell her she'd been seen, but no such call came. Everyone was too busy to notice her.

She reached a landing with a door directly ahead of her. The sound of footsteps and voices echoed along the corridor, battling with the noise of wood being sawn and nails being hammered. Footsteps from above startled her – the heavy tread of someone descending the stairs. Slipping into the room ahead, she found herself inside the real House of Wonders.

Zinnie stood still for a minute, her back against the door. Before her was a series of connected rooms that seemed to stretch on and on, one after the other, vanishing into the distance in every direction she looked. Each was lit only in the centre and with varying degrees of brightness, giving the impression of mystery. The walls, where they could be seen, had been painted a deep carmine red. The room in which she stood was lined with glass cabinets, filled with all manner of bleached skulls of unnamed monsters, accompanied by faces of all shapes, sizes and colours, every one different. At first Zinnie thought they were made of skin, that MacDuff had taken the visages from numerous once-living things and mounted them for the good people of Edinburgh to gawk at. It was only when she overcame the sudden thundering of her heart and stepped closer that she saw some of them were made of wood, others of shell or bone or cloth. They were masks, hundreds of them, assembled from who knew how many nations of the globe.

She moved on to the room beyond, which was not yet complete – some of the cabinets were still being built. Of those that were finished, some were larger than the ones that held the masks. Zinnie was shocked to see that they had straw in their bases and small shelters too, as if things unseen but living lurked within. Did Phineas MacDuff really keep creatures here, as well as ornaments from other lands? She thought of Ruby the monkey, with her little black-and-white face. Had Ruby been destined to spend her days here, penned into one of these glass cabinets? If so, no wonder Aelfine had run away. She would have wanted to save her pet from being put into a cage like this.

Zinnie moved on into the next room and found the biggest cabinet of all. It took up half the floor space and reached from floor to ceiling. There was straw strewn in the bottom of this one too, but no shelter like in the smaller enclosures. Instead, there was a tree trunk leaning at a steep angle against the rear wall, which had been made to look like a rock and that had shallow ledges jutting out of it here and there. They led up to the ceiling, into which had been hammered a series of hoops. Hanging from the ceiling, suspended on sturdy rope, were two small swings, which Zinnie gauged would be just large enough to hold a child each. The cabinet was otherwise empty, apart from two iron rings that had been hammered into either side of the cage. From these rings led chains just long enough that whatever was fastened to them would be able to climb up to each of the swings. Zinnie stared at these for a while, realizing what they meant. The cabinet had obviously been made for two occupants.

On the wall behind the swings were large painted letters. Zinnie couldn't read them, but in a sudden, horrible flash of understanding, she knew that if they were said aloud they would say THE HUMAN MONKEY. She felt sick.

"Two more ears!" boomed a loud voice behind her. "Two! It's beyond a joke!"

Zinnie jumped and turned. The voice – and the two sets of heavy footsteps that accompanied it – was in the neighbouring room and moving swiftly closer. Panicked, she looked around for somewhere to hide. There were two other cabinets in the room but both were unfinished and offered nowhere to conceal herself. The only other object in the room she had at first dismissed as a pile of carpets, probably left for use elsewhere when the house was finished. Now she realized that the haphazard fabric was actually a small draped tent. It was circular with a peaked roof, made of a heavy, glittering fabric printed with a motif of stars and moons. There was a sign standing beside it, a picture of a woman sitting before a crystal ball alongside more words she couldn't decipher.

Zinnie ran towards it and dropped to her knees, scrambling through the opening just as the footsteps arrived in the room. Shuffling backwards, she fetched up against a large wooden trunk.

"Three pairs over the past two weeks. I tell you, it's too much," the voice was saying. It was MacDuff. "I've already given you money for a job you promised you'd be able to accomplish, and so far you've given me nothing in return."

It was the second voice, though, that made her hold her breath in shock. Zinnie would know it anywhere.

"You only asked me yesterday," it said gruffly, and with no hint of apology. "I ain't a miracle worker."

Bartholomew Talbot.

"It's too much, I tell you," MacDuff went on, as if Talbot hadn't spoken. "I came to this city because I thought it was safe to stop at last, to make a home for myself. But I've had nothing but trouble since I got here. The ears, man, the ears! It must be the Queensland Kings, it must! But how did they find me? And the *ears*! I was sure it must be the fortune-teller and that it would stop once she was dealt with. Now I need *you* to deal with it. If you don't, you'll get nothing."

Zinnie couldn't make sense of anything MacDuff was saying, but it was Talbot's next words that really made her blood run cold.

"What about your missing idiot?" he asked. "Could it be her, causing trouble? Following you?"

MacDuff snorted. "She can't even look after herself. She doesn't have the gumption to cut off a man's ears and send them to me."

"But you still want her found?"

"I can't open without my crowning exhibit, can I? They're all over the posters. If I took a coin for every time I've been asked about them, I could build a bridge to the moon. Besides, she knows too much. I want her back here, under lock and key. A wild animal and a fool. Surely they can't be difficult to locate. Or is even that too much for the likes of you?"

Zinnie could hear Talbot's reply edging out between clenched teeth. She knew that if not for the promise of payment when he delivered, the villain would happily slip a knife between Phineas MacDuff's ribs there and then.

"I'll find them."

"Good. And be quick about it, I want to open the lower two levels next week while we finish the upper ones. Seeing what we've got down here will make people eager to come back for a second time once we're fully open. I'm losing money every day this place stands idle. I'm a rich man, Talbot," MacDuff added. "I'm sure I'll find frequent uses for a man of your ... skills ... in the future. Providing you can prove to me that you do actually possess the talents of which you boast."

"I'll sort out your troubles, MacDuff," Talbot growled. "Don't fret about that."

"Good. Get on with it. Now I've got affairs to set straight. See yourself out."

MacDuff's heavy footsteps stalked away. Eventually, there was the distant sound of a door opening and closing. Zinnie sat still, listening, but Talbot didn't leave. She heard him move with slow, deliberate footsteps. For a second she thought he was heading for her hiding place, that he was suddenly going to rip aside the tent's heavy entrance flap and declare that he'd known she'd been there all along. Panicked, she lifted the trunk's lid, but it was full of clothes, with no room for her to hide inside. Talbot kept walking, though, his footsteps moving to the other side of the room. Then he stopped. There was another moment of silence.

"Where are you, you wee wretch?" he said, his voice low and menacing. "I'll find you yet. I'm coming for you.

And you'll be sorry that you've led me this little dance."

It was then that Zinnie knew exactly where he was standing. He was looking into the Human Monkey's enclosure. Into *Aelfine*'s prison.

Talbot's footsteps echoed past her again and away, following MacDuff's route out.

Zinnie sat still in the darkness of the tent for a long time afterwards, trying to make sense of everything she'd seen and heard.

CHAPTER 17

Zinnie slipped out of the House of Wonders the same way she'd gone in. She was shaken and still feeling sick to her stomach. She kept an eye out for Talbot as she hurried home, but there was no sign of him. Still, he and his men would be out there somewhere. Now that she knew they were searching for Aelfine and Ruby, she was doubly afraid. Talbot was the worst man in Old Edinburgh, he knew the closes as well as Zinnie herself, and everyone – including her, though she'd never let him know it – was afraid of him. If Talbot were looking for Aelfine and Ruby, then it wouldn't be long before he found them.

Zinnie hoped that she'd get back to Mary King's Close to find their spot deserted, Sadie and Aelfine already having gone to Doctor Jex-Blake's, but that was not to be.

"I couldn't get her to come with me," Sadie said when

Zinnie reappeared. "As soon as I told her that we'd be going to see a doctor, she refused to leave. She's been hunched up in the corner like that ever since. She's terrified. I didn't want to leave her alone."

Aelfine had crammed herself in between the wall and the fireplace and pulled her knees up to her chest. Her forehead was resting on her knees and Zinnie could just see Ruby's little face peeking out beneath her mistress's chin.

"What is it she's afraid of?" Zinnie asked.

Sadie shook her head. "The doctor, I think. I tried to explain that she'd just want to help, but Aelfine burst into tears and begged me not to make her go. Did you find anything out?"

Zinnie nodded grimly. "Aye. It's worse than I thought, in more ways than one. Talbot's looking for her. Have you got something that might help to calm her? I need to ask her some things."

Sadie nodded. "I've got camomile and St John's wort. I'll brew her a tea. But I've got to get back to Nell soon…"

Zinnie squeezed her sister's arm. "I know." She wanted to visit Nell too, but she knew that while Sadie's skills lay in looking after the sick, her own would be put to better use elsewhere. "Tell her I'll come and see her as soon as I can, won't you?"

Sadie nodded and reached up to pluck two handfuls of herbs from her stores, busying herself over the fire. Zinnie went to Aelfine and settled beside the girl, pulling her legs up to mirror how she was sitting.

"Aelfine," she said quietly. "I went to the House of Wonders. I know why you ran away. You never have to go back there, I promise. It's an evil place, run by an evil man."

Aelfine hugged her knees harder to her chest, but said nothing. Ruby chattered quietly, one paw against her mistress's cheek as if trying to soothe her.

"But the thing is you can't stay here. If you do, he'll find you. So we need to get you somewhere safe. Where's home for you?"

Aelfine's shoulders shuddered as she took in a great breath. For a moment Zinnie thought she would stay silent, but then her rasping voice came out in a whisper almost too faint to hear. "*Nowhere*."

"Well," Zinnie said, trying a different tack as she watched Sadie stir the steaming cup of herbs, "what about where you were before you came here, to Edinburgh?"

"Circus," came the short reply. "With … with Ma."

Sadie and Zinnie looked at each other. "You were with your ma? Well – where is she now, Aelfine? Is she still with the circus?"

Aelfine said nothing as Sadie passed the tea to Zinnie. Then she began to cry again, great wracking sobs that tore out of her lungs as if the world were ending. "Dead," she sobbed. "Ma's dead, dead, *dead*. All alone. No one but Ruby. And he's going to kill me too."

Zinnie's blood ran cold for the second time that day. "What do you mean?"

"He hurt Ma," Aelfine sobbed. "Because she said she would tell if he didn't let us go. He put his hands on her, here." The little girl lifted her head and demonstrated with her hands round her neck. "And then she didn't get up any more."

Zinnie stared into the mug she held in her hands, her heart thumping hard. "You mean ... *Phineas MacDuff* did that?"

"My fault," Aelfine went on, still sobbing. "Because I didn't want to be a monkey. He tricked Ma. He said that he just wanted her to do her fortune-telling. So we went with him because she knew I didn't want to be in the circus any more. But then he built a cage for ... for Ruby and me."

Zinnie swallowed round the swift pounding of her heart. "Aelfine – did you see it happen? Were you there? Did he ... did you see what he did to your ma?"

"I was hiding. With Ruby."

"Did he see you?"

Aelfine nodded. "Ma told me to stay hidden. She made me promise. But, when he hurt her, I screamed. I couldn't ... keep ... it ... in. And then he knew where I was. He chased me and..."

"And you ran," Zinnie said. "You ran here."

"After."

"After what?"

"After I saw where he took Ma."

Zinnie and Sadie looked at each other.

"You mean where he went with your ma after…"

"After she was dead." Aelfine sobbed harder. "But he's looking for us, he's looking for me, because…" Her voice dissolved into a storm of sobbing again. "He still wants me to be a monkey. I heard him. He told Ma. 'She's mine,' he said. 'She's my missing link. She'll make me rich.'"

"Mother of God," Zinnie heard Sadie murmur. "This is … this is murder. Cold-blooded *murder*, Zin. We must tell the police!"

Zinnie's stomach turned over. "We can't," she said. "Not you and me. They've got posters up of me, remember? And, even if they didn't, they wouldn't take our word for it anyway, would they? Two street rats bad-mouthing a fine businessman of the New Town? We haven't got any proof!"

Sadie bit her lip. "Aelfine can go herself then," she said. "We can point her towards the police station and she can go in and tell them what she's just told us."

Zinnie looked at Aelfine, who was rocking where she sat, still sobbing, her face screwed up in distress and terror. "Do you think they'd listen to her any more than they'd listen to us?"

Sadie's face took on a despairing look. "Then what are we going to do?"

"I still think Doctor Jex-Blake is our best bet."

"No!" Aelfine moaned loudly, causing Ruby to chatter

even more. "No doctors! They'll take me away! He said so. He told Ma, if I wasn't good, that he'd let the doctors take me away!"

"Doctor Jex-Blake isn't going to take you away, Aelfine," Zinnie said in her most reassuring voice. "But we need help and she'll be able to give it to us. I know she will."

"They'll put me in a 'sylum," Aelfine moaned, her forehead against her knees again as Ruby tried to comfort her. "They will, they will. Without Ma, they'll lock me away."

Zinnie looked at Sadie. *Doctor Jex-Blake wouldn't do that*, Zinnie thought. *She's not like that.* But she didn't know the doctor, not really, and, after all, wasn't Zinnie already worried that Jex-Blake would put Nell in an orphanage rather than let her come back home to Mary King's Close? Wasn't that also the reason that Zinnie had never wanted Conan Doyle to know where they lived, either? The likes of them didn't have a say over their own lives, not once other people got involved, so how much less of a say would someone like Aelfine have, with no one that mattered to speak up for her? Aelfine's fears, she realized, weren't idle ones at all.

"No one's going to lock you away," Zinnie said quietly. "I promise. We'll find a way to keep you safe ourselves."

"But Zinnie," Sadie protested. "How on earth—"

"I don't know yet," Zinnie said, interrupting. "I've got to think. But the first thing we need to do is get Aelfine and Ruby out of Mary King's Close. She can't stay here. Sooner or later, someone will realize who she is. Talbot will already have put it about that he's looking for her."

"But if we can't take her to the doctor's…"

"There's someone who still owes me a favour," Zinnie said, standing up. "And Writers' Court will be better than here, at least."

CHAPTER 18

"You must be joking," said Constance McQuirter. "Do I look like a babysitter?"

"I'm not asking you, I'm telling you," said Zinnie, standing in Constance's room with her arms crossed. "Or you know what will happen."

McQuirter sighed, looking at the cloaked figure of Aelfine lurking by the door. Sadie stood with her, one arm round her shoulders, looking anxious. "Who is she then? What's she done that she needs to hide?"

Zinnie glanced over her shoulder, but Aelfine's face was still covered by her hood.

Constance gave a short laugh. "Oh, come on. It's another little sister you've adopted, isn't it? As if all these waifs and strays count as family."

Zinnie gritted her teeth. "It's none of your business.

All you need to do is let her stay here and keep quiet about it. I mean it, Constance – not a word to anyone. Or first thing tomorrow you'll find yourself begging for your breakfast or else in a jail cell."

The woman huffed for another minute, as if trying to come up with an argument. Then she sighed and nodded. "All right. But I've got to go out. I'm visiting a client."

"All the better. See? This is going to work out just fine."

"If you say so," Constance muttered, eyeing Aelfine's shrouded figure with suspicion and curiosity.

"Just forget there's anyone here at all, Constance," Zinnie advised her, as Sadie hugged Aelfine and murmured to her.

Constance snorted and turned away to pick up a shawl as Zinnie spoke to Aelfine.

"Don't worry," she said. "Everything's going to be fine. Just stay quiet – I know you can do that – and don't go anywhere. I'll be back before you know it. All right?"

Aelfine's hood nodded up and down. Zinnie hugged her lightly.

"Do you really think we can trust Constance not to gossip?" Sadie asked, once the two girls were back outside.

"Usually, I'd say no," Zinnie admitted. "But she knows that her livelihood depends on her keeping quiet. She'll play along, at least for now."

Sadie nodded. "Back to the doctor's then?" she asked. "We've been away from Nell for too long."

Zinnie took her sister's hand. "You go. There's somewhere else I need to be first."

"But Zinnie—"

"I know," Zinnie said. "I'll come soon, I promise. But I've got to find a way to solve Aelfine's problem if I want to keep us all safe, and I think that means bringing MacDuff to justice. Trust me," she said, when Sadie looked alarmed, before digging in her pocket and pulling out the crown she'd got back from Constance the day before. "Take this for food and go. I'll join you as soon as I can, I promise. Give Nell a kiss from me."

Conan Doyle had not long returned from the Royal Infirmary when Zinnie was shown into his study. He was sitting in an armchair beside the window, rifling through a broadsheet. He looked up when his butler showed her in.

"Aha, Miss Zinnie. It's fortuitous that you should choose to call at this moment, as I was just going to come and find you. There's been a development."

"I know. You've had another earless body."

Conan Doyle stood up, a look of consternation on his face. "But how on earth could you know that?"

"Because I know where the ears were sent. To Phineas MacDuff."

The frown on Conan Doyle's face deepened as he searched

121

his memory. "You mean … the owner of that new place on George Street? The one who was at Lady Sarah's seance?"

"The very same."

"That can't be right," said the medical student. "If he was the one being plagued by such grotesquery – if he was being *sent* them, deliberately – he'd have taken the matter to the police and there would be a report of it in one of these –" he shook the newspaper still in his hand – "and there has been not a whisper of it. I would know if there had been. I've checked. Frequently."

Zinnie shook her head. "I don't think he would have taken it to the police. I don't think Phineas MacDuff is what he seems."

"What do you mean? How do you know any of this anyway?"

"I … went to the House of Wonders. To have a look around."

"What? But it's not open yet!"

Zinnie shrugged. "Maybe not for you toffs…"

"I am *not* a toff," Conan Doyle said in an affronted voice.

"All right, man-with-his-own-carriage," she said. "Do you want to hear about this or not?"

Conan Doyle sighed and sat back down again, waving her into the chair opposite. "Very well. Might as well tell me what you know, I suppose."

Zinnie took a seat and chewed her lip for a minute as she tried to work out how to proceed without bringing

Aelfine into the conversation. "It's a horrible place," she said. "There are all sorts of terrible things in there."

Conan Doyle crossed his legs and steepled his fingers. "Well, other cultures can seem strange to the uneducated mind," he said.

"It wasn't the masks or anything like that," Zinnie said, trying and failing to keep a scathing note out of her voice. "He's got living things too. Things in cages."

"So it's a zoo as well." Conan Doyle shrugged. "That makes sense. He's travelled extensively – it's not surprising he's collected live specimens."

"No, that's not—" Zinnie stopped. She'd been about to say that she thought he had *people* in there too, but the only one she actually knew about was Aelfine.

"Tell me about the ears," Conan Doyle prompted. "What makes you think MacDuff is the one who received them?"

"Because I heard him say so." She relayed the exchange she had overheard between MacDuff and Talbot.

"How strange," Conan Doyle said with a frown, staring out of the window. "Perhaps someone brought them to him, knowing that he's interested in … unusual items. They might have thought he would pay money to add them to his collection."

"No," said Zinnie. "That definitely wasn't it."

Conan Doyle frowned. "I know I suggested finding alternative help in recovering what he'd lost. But why wouldn't he go to the police over the ears?"

"I think he's a crook," Zinnie said. "And a crook wouldn't ask the police for help, would he?"

"A crook? Why would you say that? Just because he's a collector of things you don't understand doesn't mean—"

"He's a murderer."

"What?" Conan Doyle spluttered. "That's preposterous!"

"Why? Because you ate a fancy dinner with him at some lady's house?"

"No, of course not, that's not..." Conan Doyle sighed. "Just tell me what makes you think such a thing."

"He said that he'd originally thought the ears were sent by the fortune-teller that worked for him, and that they'd stop arriving when she'd been 'dealt' with, but they hadn't. I think he killed her because he thought she was sending him the ears as a message."

"What, just because she's gone off somewhere you think she's dead? That's absurd," Conan Doyle said hotly. "It's more likely that she left of her own accord. She probably just joined a circus – people in such professions move around a lot. Perhaps she didn't like staying in one place."

"But that's not what it sounded like," Zinnie said, desperately trying to think of a way to convince him without revealing Aelfine's existence. "It sounded as if he'd been the one to make her disappear. If he thought she was the one sending the ears as a message, he must have also thought she knew something about him that he didn't want anyone else to know. Something really bad. Something that would make him want to get rid of her."

Conan Doyle sighed. "This is all just conjecture, Miss Zinnie, and very wild conjecture at that. We don't even know that this woman's dead. There's no evidence of that, is there?"

Zinnie thought of what Aelfine had told them, that she knew where her mother's body lay. A corpse would count as evidence surely? But how could Zinnie lead Conan Doyle there without revealing how she knew where and who it was?

"I'm more interested in why MacDuff has been receiving severed ears," Conan Doyle mused, oblivious to Zinnie's thoughts. "And, moreover, why he's employed this Talbot person instead of going to the police. That certainly smacks of wanting to conceal something."

Zinnie swallowed her frustration. "Did you make those sketches?" she asked. "Of the men without their ears?"

"I did." Conan Doyle rose and went to his desk, pulling out his notebooks as Zinnie joined him. "They're in here. Why, what are you thinking?"

"Not sure. Something else I heard MacDuff say."

"All right," Conan Doyle said, laying out the sketches before her. "What is it?"

Zinnie examined each drawing. "These are exactly what the bodies looked like?"

"As close as I could get them," Conan Doyle told her. "I'm no artist, I'm afraid."

Zinnie pointed to a series of scars across each of

the dead men's chests. They were linked together in haphazard semicircles.

"Are those the burns you told me about?" Zinnie asked, pointing to the scars. "Where you think they each tried to remove a tattoo?"

"Yes, indeed. I think they're burn or scorch marks, perhaps from a cattle brand."

"Why would anyone do that?"

Conan Doyle shrugged. "I think they each bore the same tattoo, and these marks were left when they tried to erase them. They were doing it in a rush. There are the remains of black marks beneath still visible, you see? Not enough to work out what was there unfortunately. They did a good job of wiping out whatever they didn't want anyone else to see. But the shape left behind says to me that each of the men had the same tattoo, so they probably at least knew each other."

Zinnie looked at the sketches for another moment. Then she picked up a pencil and found a clean corner of paper.

"What are you doing?" Conan Doyle asked.

Zinnie didn't answer. She looked at each of the three sketches again and copied just the marks sticking out from beneath the first burn. When she joined the marks from the three different sketches together in her single drawing, the result looked like most of a circle with a little angled strike through on the bottom curve. Zinnie leaned back and looked at it.

"Great Scott!" Conan Doyle exclaimed.

"I'm not good with letters," Zinnie said. "Never was, even when I was wee. But I always got one right. The Q. Because I liked what it looked like and I liked the sound it makes. That looks like it could be a Q to me. What about you?"

Conan Doyle nodded. "I think you're right. Let's see what other letters we can come up with."

Not many was the answer. But they did come up with what might have been an E, a K and a G.

"That was a truly stunning piece of deductive reasoning, Miss Zinnie," Conan Doyle said. "But I'm not sure it's much help to us, in the end."

Zinnie handed him the pencil. "Can you write something down? Two words: 'Queensland Kings'."

He frowned but did as he was told. "What's that got to do with anything?"

"Could that be what the tattoos said?"

Conan Doyle considered and then nodded. "Perhaps. Why?"

"MacDuff was talking about them, but I don't know what they are. The Queensland Kings, he said. And, at the seance, he kept asking about kings, didn't he? He wanted to know if any of them were there in the spirit realm – if any of them were dead."

Conan Doyle frowned. "But Queensland is in Australia. MacDuff is American; when Lady Sarah was putting him in his place about travelling, he said he'd never been to Australia. What connection could there be?"

Zinnie shrugged. "I'm just telling you what I heard."

Conan Doyle set his jaw. "Well, Miss Zinnie," he said. "It must mean something. There is clearly a game afoot and I am determined to find out what it is. Leave this with me. I'll make some enquiries."

CHAPTER 19

"She's a tough one," Doctor Jex-Blake told Zinnie, as they stood outside Nell's sickroom. "And lucky too. It's bronchitis, not consumption. If it had been the latter, there would have been nothing I could do to save her. Still, I honestly didn't think your sister had much of a chance, but thanks to Sadie's ministrations and Nell's strong will, it looks as if she might pull through. There's a long way to go yet, mind. Her fever has broken but her lungs are still congested. However, we are hopeful that we can clear them."

Relief left Zinnie light-headed. Through the open door, she could see Sadie standing at Nell's bedside. Nell had a towel over her head, concealing both her face and the steaming bowl that Sadie was holding under her nose.

"I'm glad you're here, Zinnie," the doctor went on.

"Will you come with me for a moment or two? There's something I'd like to discuss with you."

Zinnie followed as Jex-Blake led her down the hallway. Her fingers clutched the money left in her pocket – Zinnie assumed this conversation would be about payment for Nell's care. It took her by surprise then that, when the doctor pushed open a door, it revealed a small parlour where Lady Sarah Montague was sipping tea from a china cup.

"Miss Zinnie!" Lady Sarah exclaimed, as Jex-Blake ushered her inside. "How lovely it is to see you again. I'm so glad to hear that your littlest sister seems to be on the mend."

"Thank you, Lady Sarah," Zinnie said, as Doctor Jex-Blake moved past her and took her own chair. The two women glanced at each other and Zinnie felt a horrible sinking feeling in her stomach. Nothing good ever came of adults sharing looks like that. She pulled out the coins. "I can pay now."

Doctor Jex-Blake smiled. "There's no need, Zinnie. Lady Sarah has already covered the costs incurred."

"I – why would you do that?" Zinnie stammered, her surprise making her rude.

Lady Sarah waved a hand as she took a sip of her tea. "It was nothing, Zinnie. The least I could do. I have a lot of money and I spend much of it on what could be considered extreme frivolity when one understands the troubles to be found on your side of Edinburgh. Meeting you and your sisters has made me aware that I really could do more in that respect. Which is what Doctor Jex-Blake and I have been discussing."

Zinnie's heart sank further still. "We don't need help, if that's what you're going to say. We're fine."

"Zinnie," the doctor said gently. "You've done a marvellous job in helping two children who would otherwise have suffered horribly, and been all alone in doing so. But you're not 'fine'. None of you are. Look at Nell. That place you live in – it's not fit for a child. And really, my dear, you're still a child yourself. How old are you?"

"Fourteen," Zinnie lied, but the doctor's look told her she hadn't been believed. The cold clutch of fear tightened its grip round her heart. "You can't take them away. You can't lock them up."

"No one's talking about locking anyone up," Lady Sarah said in a soothing voice. "I know of several wonderful institutions—"

"Not an orphanage," Zinnie said in full-fledged panic. "I won't let you put Nell in one of those places."

"But she'd be looked after well. She'd be fed, cared for and—"

"Cared for?" Zinnie asked. "Mr Conan Doyle couldn't even be sure that his hospital would look after her!"

Doctor Jex-Blake looked away. "It was far more expedient to bring her here, Zinnie."

"Because *you* didn't care about the colour of her skin,"

Zinnie pressed. "You and Lady Sarah and Mr Conan Doyle – none of you do. But how many people can you vouch for who would be the same?"

There was a brief silence.

"I don't think that's—" Lady Sarah began, but Zinnie cut her off once more.

"You don't *know*," Zinnie said fiercely. "You've never even been inside one, have you? I have. And I'd never let you put either of my sisters there. The only place Nell's going is home with me and Sadie. I'll look after her. I'll look after both of them, just like I always have."

"Zinnie—"

Whatever Jex-Blake had been about to say was cut off by the maid opening the door and offering a quick curtsey. "Beg pardon, ma'am, but there's a policeman here to talk to you. Constable Roberts. It's about the missing milk."

"I'll leave," Zinnie said.

"Wait, please," said the doctor. "This will only take a moment. Mary, show the policeman in."

Zinnie edged towards the door, unwilling to be in the same room as the law, given that the law had plastered her face – or something that looked a lot like her face – all over the Old Town of Edinburgh.

"Beg pardon, Miss Jex-Blake, for disturbing you," said the copper, as he came through the door. "I just need to check—"

Zinnie winced as she recognized the portly figure of

the constable whose shin she had kicked to allow them to escape as they'd taken back the pocket watch. She turned her face away, hoping that he wouldn't notice her, but Lady Luck really didn't seem to be on her side at the moment.

"'Ere," said Constable Roberts. "Don't I know you, lad?"

Zinnie made a run for it, darting into action and round him before he had a chance to react. His shout of surprise echoed behind her as she flung open the door.

"You! Stop him! He's a thief!"

Zinnie glanced at the front door but realized she'd never get it open in time. She ran deeper into the house instead.

"What's been stolen, Constable?" she heard Lady Sarah cry, as they followed.

"Silver pocket watch from a pawnbroker's on Bread Street," Roberts puffed, already out of breath. "What's he doing here?"

"I treat all sorts," said Doctor Jex-Blake.

"Got his fellow thieves here as well then?" Roberts shouted. "There's three wanted, him and two girls."

Zinnie slewed through an open door into an empty room and stopped dead, listening. She'd give herself up now if it meant Sadie and Nell were safe.

"No," said the doctor. "No, definitely not."

Zinnie breathed a sigh of relief, and then spied a way out. She ran across the room and hauled up the window. It looked out on to the neat garden. A moment later, Zinnie was out, running across the small lawn. She heard another shout as she scrambled atop the high brick wall at the other end and looked back to see the copper leaning out of the window. They both knew there was no chance he'd follow her, not that way.

"I'll get you yet, lad, just see if I don't!" he shouted. "Come back to this place and I'll have you, that's for sure."

Zinnie dropped out of sight and was gone.

CHAPTER 20

Zinnie ran back to the Royal Mile, her heart pounding in her chest. What must Doctor Jex-Blake and Lady Sarah think of her? She was grateful, at least, that they hadn't given her up, which made her think that they'd keep Sadie and Nell from the law too. Zinnie could only hope that the door to Nell's room would remain shut while Constable Roberts was inside the clinic walls. He wouldn't think to question the word of the two ladies, but just a glimpse of either Sadie or Nell – and especially of them together – and even the flattest-footed of coppers would realize what he was seeing. She was relieved too that neither the doctor nor Lady Sarah had seen fit to correct the fact that he'd called her a boy.

What now, though? She couldn't go back to the clinic, at least not right away. Roberts would be on the lookout for her. She'd hurt his pride, after all, not once but twice now. She thought briefly about going to Conan Doyle and asking him to explain to the police what she'd been doing with the pocket watch, but dismissed that notion immediately. She could well imagine the medical student's expression when he realized she'd willingly become a criminal on his behalf. She wasn't entirely sure he would help her once he knew, and it likely wouldn't make a difference anyway. No, that wasn't something she—

The attack came out of nowhere. A large hand grabbed her by the throat, dragging her into a shadowed alley and lifting her into the air. A second later, Zinnie found herself up against the wall, choking, scrabbling at Bartholomew Talbot's rough fingers. She kicked out, desperate for breath, but she might as well have been fighting a rock.

"Well, well, well," he said in a soft voice, eyeing her struggles with utter disdain. "Where are you running to so fast, my wee lamb?"

Zinnie went for her knife but her vision was blurring. He saw her shaking hand coming and knocked the blade from her grip with his free hand.

"I ain't gonna kill you," he said, loosening his grip just enough to let her slump against the wall, gasping. "Leastways, not yet."

Zinnie coughed, dragging in breath after breath through her crushed throat. Then she kicked out again, but he was ready for her. Talbot dodged the lash of her foot and replaced his grip on her neck, this time lifting her clear off the ground. Stars exploded behind her eyes, a dense black cloud gathering at the edges of her vision.

"None of that," Talbot whispered, his lips against her ear. "I just want some information, that's all. Word on the closes is that you've adopted another scrag of wasteling meat. Now who could that be, I wonder?"

Zinnie couldn't have answered him even if she'd wanted to.

I'm going to die, she thought. *He's going to kill me, right now, and no one will even notice. Least of all him.*

She wasn't sad about it exactly. Death suddenly felt as if it might be quite a calm, quiet place to be, away from the heavy burden that it seemed to be just to live.

But what about Sadie, and Nell? What about Aelfine? Who would look after them if you were gone?

The thought brought her round, just a little. Zinnie struggled against Talbot's hand and he seemed to realize that she wasn't faking. It was likely more to do with the information he wanted than any worry about killing her, but he let her go, just enough for her to find her feet and take another desperate breath.

"She's no one," Zinnie spluttered hoarsely.

Talbot loomed over her, hand pressing hard against her thin shoulder, almost threatening to shatter the bone. "Must have been someone, lamb."

Zinnie shook her head, her throat aching. "Didn't even

know her name. Just a runaway. And she … ran away again, once she'd eaten our food and nicked our money."

"Freak, was she? Something strange about her?"

Zinnie frowned. "What? No. Just had the mark of the pox, that's all."

"Animal with her? A pet?"

Zinnie actually managed to fake a laugh. "A pet? She couldn't even feed herself. Though I s'pose she can now, what with the coins she nabbed."

Talbot leaned in, narrowing his eyes as he examined hers, as if he could read the truth there. His breath smelled of whisky and rot. Zinnie felt sick but she didn't look away. He grinned.

"What did I tell you when I first took you in?" he said. "Never trust no one, never help no one, cos there's no one down here who's not looking out for themselves. Surprised you ain't been done over before, with your do-gooding."

Zinnie coughed again and wriggled free, forcing herself to stay upright as she tried to catch her breath, despite her legs feeling like jelly. She'd long ago vowed never to look beaten in front of Talbot.

He'd been the first person she'd met as a runaway bairn, trying to find somewhere to sleep. At first he'd masqueraded as a good sort wanting to help her. He'd taken her in, told his gang to look after her, make sure she was fed. But what he'd wanted in return was a slave who would steal for him, a small body with little fingers who could get into places and pockets more easily than he or any of his other brutes. She'd run from the orphanage because it had been no better than a prison, but with Talbot she'd found herself in another sort of prison, one that led to far worse punishments. Zinnie had freed herself just as soon as she could – she'd learned to stand up for herself, to fight back fiercely enough that in the end Talbot had decided she was more trouble than she was worth. But he never let her think she'd escaped him for good. It was Talbot who had taught her every bad thing she knew. He was also the reason that Zinnie had vowed to herself that she would pluck every lone child she could out of the gutter herself, before he could get to them.

Talbot watched her. "You're a tough one, I'll give you that," he said, with a grudging kind of respect. "Could have made real use of you."

Her head was pounding and her throat must already be black and blue, but Zinnie made herself look him in the eye with her chin up. Talbot took a step back, rain peppering his greasy hair.

"Guess I'll have to keep looking then, lamb," he said softly. "She's out there somewhere."

He turned and sauntered away into the bustle of the Mile, whistling to himself and nodding nonchalantly to a passer-by who stood in the shadows, a man Zinnie didn't recognize who wore a wide-brimmed hat tipped low over one ear. She leaned back against the wall, gulping more air and letting the cool rain fall on her face. She wasn't fool enough to think Talbot had taken her story at face value. Like he'd said, he never trusted anyone. He'd be watching her, just in case.

Zinnie shut her eyes, trying to think. Where would she be safe? Where would Aelfine be safe? They couldn't stay in Constance's room – it was probably her who'd gossiped about Zinnie's new 'sister' in the first place. Even if it wasn't, it wouldn't be long before Constance realized that all she needed to do to get rid of both of them was shop Zinnie to the coppers. No one would believe Zinnie's side of the story and she'd never get to anyone who could prove what she had to say before the police caught her.

There was only one place for her and Aelfine now.

CHAPTER 21

"I'm sorry that we've ended up back down here," Zinnie said, keeping her voice quiet in case of echoes. "But I don't know where else to go. There won't be any people here — they're all still afraid of the ghost."

"I don't mind," Aelfine said, still shrouded in her cloak as they made their way through one of the dingy rooms close to where Zinnie had first found her. "No people is better."

Zinnie was still shaken after her flight from Grove Street and her horrible run-in with Talbot, but the deeper they got into Mary King's Close, the calmer she became. The place was still deserted. A cold dark ruin it might be but at least they'd hear anyone coming for them. She wished she could get word to Sadie not to come back home. Her sister would be worried, she knew, but Zinnie hoped she had the sense to stay put with Nell – assuming Doctor Jex-Blake didn't turn her out, of course.

A muted chattering came from beneath Aelfine's cloak.

"I think you can let Ruby out now," Zinnie said. "The poor thing must be tired of being under there."

Aelfine opened her cloak and the monkey jumped down from where she'd been clinging round her waist. Ruby stretched her arms and then ran lightly up to sit on Aelfine's shoulder, her tail curling round her mistress's neck as she muttered in her own little language. She watched Zinnie with strangely wise eyes.

"Is that why you pretended to be a ghost in the first place?" Zinnie asked, her candle casting their faces into strange patterns of shadow as they started moving again. "To scare people away?"

Aelfine nodded. "I just wanted Ruby and me to be safe."

"How did you do it? I really thought it was a spirit come to haunt me."

The girl bit her lip, as if she didn't want to speak. "I learned it at the circus."

"OK," Zinnie said. "So it was a sideshow? And the person who did it showed you how to make the ghost?"

Aelfine shook her head. "No one was supposed to know how," she said. "But I hid and watched. I'm good at hiding. Then I asked Ruby to help me."

Zinnie stopped again. "You mean you learned how to do it yourself, just from watching? That's very clever."

Aelfine shrugged, as if she weren't used to praise. They had reached the room with the fallen floor. Zinnie held out her candle, careful not to step over the edge of the void.

"Well, here we are," she said softly. "This is as far as we can go."

"No," Aelfine said. "There's more rooms. Over there."

She pointed into the darkness on the other side of the gaping hole. Ruby chattered in agreement.

"I can't get over there," Zinnie said. "There's no floor, Aelfine. There's nothing to walk on and I can't climb the way you can." She looked at the girl thoughtfully for a moment. "The ghost was floating in mid-air. It was ... see-through. I know it was you, but – *how*?"

Aelfine looked at Ruby for a moment. The monkey leaned forward to jabber in her ear and Zinnie once again found herself wondering whether Ruby understood every word, spoken or silent.

"We can show you the ghost again," Aelfine said hesitantly. "If you like."

Zinnie looked into the thick darkness. Even with her candle flaring brightly in her hand, it felt as if she could be swallowed up by it, as if it were a very real, very hungry beast just waiting to pounce. The thought of seeing the ghost again unsettled her, even though she knew it wasn't real. But it wouldn't hurt to revive the spectre if it meant scaring away anyone who'd been thinking about coming back down into these parts. There was something lurking at the edge of her mind too, the faint spark of an idea that had something to do with MacDuff, the 'ghost' and helping Aelfine, though Zinnie couldn't quite catch hold of the wisp.

"Yes," she decided. "Show it to me again."

Aelfine smiled. "Stay here."

With that, Ruby jumped from her shoulder and scampered away, Aelfine following close behind. They vanished into the darkness with nothing but the sound of quiet feet until even that grew too faint to hear. Then there was only silence. Zinnie was all alone. She tried to follow their progress but it seemed to her that the two of them had walked straight out into thin air, over the void and through the veil that separated this world from the next one, if indeed it really did exist. She found herself holding her breath.

Then came that hideous screech, as if the mouth of hell had opened and a demon had clawed its way out. Zinnie knew it was only Ruby, but in the darkness the noise took on a truly terrible quality. It moved too – for a moment, it was above her, then behind her, then to the left, to the right. It swelled close, as if near enough to touch her, and then plunged away again. The hairs on the back of Zinnie's neck stood on end, her heart pounding in her chest.

It's Ruby, she told herself, hands clenched into fists. *It's just the monkey, that's all.* But it was no good. The fear sank in, as deep as her bones.

Then the ghost itself flickered into life. If there had been a floor, it would have been dancing above it, insubstantial and barely there. It glowed faintly, the light growing and then dimming again as Ruby's demon screams went on and on. The figure lifted its arms, spreading its cloak. Zinnie cringed back as the ghostly hands seemed to reach for her across the void. Beneath the hood Zinnie could see Aelfine's mouth, stretched open wide as that scream came yet again. The effect was so entirely convincing that Zinnie had to force herself not to turn tail and run. She made herself look at the spectre, to trace its outline and stare at that screaming mouth, but try as she might Zinnie could not see how it was at all possible that it was not a real ghost, but Aelfine.

It felt as if she'd been staring at the ghoul for hours, but she knew it was really only a minute or two before the ghost's hands finally retracted beneath its cloak. That seemed to be the signal for the howling to stop and in another second the spectre had blinked out of existence again, taking its glow with it and leaving nothing but a silence so absolute that Zinnie's ears hurt.

Zinnie stayed where she was until the sound of those quiet footsteps echoed towards her once again, and then there was Aelfine with Ruby on her shoulder, both of them very much made of flesh and blood.

"I still don't see," Zinnie said, slightly breathless, when Aelfine stood in front of her again. "How did you learn to do that, just by watching?"

Aelfine made a face. "Everyone thinks I don't understand," she said. "Because of –" she waved her hand to indicate herself – "but I do."

Ruby suddenly stood up on her hind legs on Aelfine's shoulder, as stiff and alert as a bloodhound as she looked towards the tangle of rooms they had clambered through after leaving the close.

"What is it?" Zinnie whispered. "Did Ruby hear something?"

Ruby stayed still for another moment and then twisted her head round to chatter something in Aelfine's ear. Zinnie didn't need to speak the little creature's language to understand Ruby's urgency.

"Quick," she said. "Go and hide."

Aelfine darted forward and grabbed Zinnie's hand. "You come too!"

"I can't," Zinnie told her. "I don't think I'll be able to follow where you go, Aelfine. I'll be fine. Go!"

She pulled her hand out of the girl's and gave her a little push. Zinnie waited until their footsteps had faded into the darkness and then strained to hear what Ruby's sharp ears had picked up. At first she could detect nothing at all but then she picked out a sound in the darkness. It was faint but growing louder.

Someone was definitely coming. Perhaps more than one person. Talbot? Could he truly have found them so quickly?

Zinnie withdrew further into the room. Most of the

floor had gone but there was a vague pathway of surviving floorboards against one wall. They curved in a semicircle to the nearest corner, a solid spur that widened at its extremity and that could perhaps be trusted if she were careful. Zinnie crept along it, worried about going too fast and putting her foot against a rotten board. But the sounds behind her were growing louder by the minute and, if she didn't blow her candle out soon, whoever it was would see the glow.

Zinnie swallowed her fear and blew out the flame. The black mouth of the dark monster around her rushed in, and for a moment panic gripped her throat as hard as Talbot's hand had earlier. She sucked in a breath, trying not to make a sound. Then she dropped to her knees and scrambled backwards, away from the void that seemed to be pulsing cold air up and over its jagged edge. She came to the wall and pressed herself against it, even as it crumbled and flaked against her weight.

Zinnie could hear the footsteps now, growing louder every second. She held her breath.

CHAPTER 22

A light bloomed in the darkness. It was stronger than a candle flame: an oil lamp. The yellow glow drew nearer, along with the sound of footsteps and the scattering of broken bricks. Zinnie braced herself against the wall. A moment later, a single figure entered the room and stopped short.

"Watch your step here," it called back over its shoulder. "The floor has gone. I tell you, this is quite as hazardous as the ruined temples of old Khartoum."

"Lady Sarah!" Zinnie stood up in astonishment. "What are *you* doing here?"

"Good grief!" the lady said, almost jumping out of her skin. Then: "Zinnie! *There* you are! Sophia! I have found her!"

There was the sound of more footsteps and Doctor Jex-Blake also appeared in the doorway, carrying her own lamp.

Zinnie glanced across the void, afraid that the explosion of light would illuminate Aelfine's hiding place, but the further edge was still in heavy darkness.

"Zinnie," the doctor said with evident relief. "It *is* you."

"Where's Sadie?" Zinnie asked, not seeing her sister with them and fearing that she was already in custody.

"She felt it best that she remain with Nell," said Lady Sarah.

"Did you bring the police?" Zinnie asked, still staying where she was, just in case.

"The *police*?" said Lady Sarah. "No, of course we didn't. Although you really should come over here so that we can talk quietly, child, or we might as well have summoned the law, after all."

Zinnie hesitated.

"We're not going to give you or your sisters up," the doctor said softly. "We want to help. Have we not already done so? You can trust us, Zinnie."

Zinnie weighed her options and saw that, really, she had no choice.

"That's better," Lady Sarah said, as she came closer. "What an extraordinary world you have brought me to, Zinnie. Quite spectacular. I had no idea. You were right – I was utterly unaware of what was in my own city. Remiss of me, to call myself an explorer and yet be so ignorant of what was directly under my nose."

Zinnie looked Lady Sarah up and down. There was

149

something odd about her and it took her a moment to realize what. She wasn't in one of her fine dresses but was wearing what seemed to be a long tunic over men's trousers. Lady Sarah laughed a little at Zinnie's expression.

"It's a Hawaiian riding dress," she said. "Isabella Bird, the explorer, wears one so she can ride astride a saddle, as a man does. I had my seamstress make a set for me, for travelling, though with a shorter tunic. Isabella still likes to wear a skirt as much as she can, but I am always pleased to have an excuse not to. I had a fancy this would be useful attire down here. I was right, wasn't I?" She seemed pleased with herself.

"You shouldn't have come here," Zinnie said. "It's not safe."

"You're here," Doctor Jex-Blake pointed out.

"I belong here," Zinnie told her. "That's different."

The doctor looked as if she might say something about no one belonging all the way down here, but she didn't. Zinnie realized that she was eyeing her neck and wondered what Jex-Blake was looking at.

"What happened to you, Zinnie?" the doctor asked. "Are those … bruises?"

Zinnie touched her fingers to the skin that Talbot's cruel fingers had crushed. She avoided Jex-Blake's gaze. "Just dirt. Don't get much chance for a bath down here."

The doctor narrowed her eyes. She obviously didn't believe that explanation. "Tell me about the police. Is what

Constable Roberts said true? Did you steal a watch?"

"No. Well, yes, but – it wasn't like that."

"What do you mean?"

"I was taking it back. To the real owner. It *was* stolen but not by us, not first off anyway. No one's going to believe that, though, are they?"

Lady Sarah frowned. "How did you know who the watch really belonged to?"

Zinnie hesitated. "Mr Conan Doyle. He knew it had been stolen and asked us to find it."

"Arthur?" Lady Sarah said. "But then he can vouch for you, and all will be well."

"He doesn't know that we found it in a pawnbroker's shop. If he did, he probably wouldn't approve."

"Yes, well, thank heaven for small mercies," Lady Sarah said dryly. "I do love the dear boy, but he can also be exasperating. Getting street children to do his dirty work for him? I never heard the like!"

"We're good at it!" Zinnie said hotly. "And, if he knew *how* we did what we do sometimes, he might not employ us again and then we'd be worse off than we are now."

The doctor sighed. "Zinnie…"

"And don't you start talking about orphanages again," Zinnie said, cutting her off. "That's going nowhere. Nell belongs with Sadie and me."

"And what about Sadie?" Jex-Blake asked.

"What *about* Sadie?"

"She wouldn't have to go into the poorhouse," the doctor explained patiently. "She can come to me. I intend to start up a school for women who want to train in medicine. Sadie has already shown an aptitude for the profession and her knowledge of medicinal plants is unsurpassed."

"And, with both your sisters looked after, you will be free to take up the position I offered you in my household," Lady Sarah concluded. "Surely that would be better than bedding down in this place and doing odd – *very* odd – jobs for a medical student who will likely leave the city once he's qualified anyway?"

Zinnie stared at Lady Sarah. She hadn't even thought that far ahead.

"I don't—"

At that moment Ruby's haunting wail rose out of the darkness, soaring into a hellish scream that tore at Zinnie's eardrums. She winced at the sound – Aelfine must have decided it would be best to scare these new visitors away just as she had the rest of the residents. The two women paled in the light of their oil lamps.

"What the blazes is *that*?" whispered Lady Sarah, horrified.

Across the void, the glow of Aelfine's ghost swelled into uncertain being. It seemed even more otherworldly than before and Zinnie realized she was seeing it as if for the first time, through the two women's eyes. They both drew in a sharp breath as the spectre flickered before them.

"Good God!" exclaimed Lady Sarah.

"But – what is it?" asked the doctor. "What … what can it *be*?"

"It's a spirit! A true spirit, in the raw! Oh, my poor, unhappy ghost," said Lady Sarah. "What is it that you need to tell us? What has made you unable to rest, that you must wander so?"

Zinnie looked between Aelfine's spectre to Lady Sarah's earnest face and Doctor Jex-Blake's astonished expression. That wisp of an idea that had been floating about in her head for hours finally came within her grasp and, as Zinnie took hold of it, she knew exactly what she had to do.

CHAPTER 23

"You don't look like you," Aelfine whispered, as Zinnie finished changing.

"I don't feel like me, either," Zinnie grumbled, draping the old shawl over her head and gathering it round her shoulders before rearranging the skirt. "But if it means I can go about my business without being recognized, I'll have to put up with it."

Zinnie had finally managed to persuade the two ladies to leave Mary King's Close and return to the safety of their own world, with the promise that she would think about what they'd said. Lady Sarah appeared confident that she could find a solution to the girls being wanted by the police, although Zinnie herself was less hopeful. People of Lady Sarah's class always seemed to think that because they rarely experienced problems themselves, an unsolved one of someone else's had simply not been examined with due diligence.

After their departure, Zinnie had slipped back to her corner of the close and gathered up as many of their blankets as she could carry. She had tried to make Aelfine and Ruby go back to their secret place on the other side of the broken floor, but Aelfine had refused unless Zinnie were to go too. She was so tired that the idea of crossing that void, even with Aelfine's guidance, had seemed doubly impossible. Instead, they had all slept behind a pile of debris, Zinnie dozing fitfully as she attempted to keep one ear open for any sign of further intrusion.

With the blankets had come Sadie's old dress. She'd grown out of it, so the sisters had been keeping it for Nell. It was far too small for Zinnie, but she could at least get it on and, with the shawl over her head, the fact that the shoulders were definitely not in the right place was covered up. At any rate, she looked like a girl, rather than the threadbare boy that was on the police posters.

"You must go back over there while I'm gone," Zinnie said, nodding towards the other side of the hole in the floor. "You and Ruby can carry the blankets, can't you? Stay out of sight. I'll be back as soon as I can."

To Zinnie's surprise, Aelfine darted forward and wrapped her arms round Zinnie's middle, hugging her hard. She hugged the girl back with a smile.

"Thank you," said Aelfine. "I've never had a sister before."

Ruby, standing at their feet, chattered somewhat indignantly.

"Apart from Ruby," Aelfine amended.

"When I get back," Zinnie said, "I think you're going to have to show me exactly how you two make the ghost. All right?"

Aelfine nodded. "We'll show you. You'll have to go across there –" she pointed to the void – "but we'll help you. Won't we?"

Ruby tipped her head to one side and babbled her agreement.

"Right," said Zinnie, feeling her stomach drop to her toes. "Well, one thing at a time. Let's see what Conan Doyle has to say first."

When she reached the house on Picardy Place, Zinnie found Conan Doyle in his study.

"Give me a moment, please," he murmured, his brow furrowed in concentration as he bent over his desk, pen in hand. "Just want to get this down…"

Zinnie pulled the shawl from her head as she waited. A few minutes later, Conan Doyle dabbed his pen on the paper decisively and then laid it down, looking up at her with a smile.

"My apologies, Miss Zinnie," he said. "I have had my

first story accepted for print, you know. It is to be called *The Mystery of Sasassa Valley*. It will be published without my name attached to it – I'm not sure I want the world to know I write stories in my spare time – but it is a satisfying feeling, I must say. Still, the tale I have to tell you now is, I confess, perhaps even more exciting."

"You've found something out about MacDuff?"

"I have indeed. Come, take a seat and I shall tell you a story of dastardly behaviour at the far ends of the earth."

Zinnie did as she was told, settling into one of the chairs by the window while Conan Doyle remained at his desk. He passed her a piece of paper. It looked as if it had been cut from a newspaper and was beginning to yellow at the edges. Big letters formed words over the top of two columns of smaller text accompanied by a picture of a locomotive. The train seemed to be tipped almost on its side. On the horizon loomed huge, snow-capped mountains.

"That," said Conan Doyle, "is from an edition of the *Scotsman* that was printed in 1867. I asked a friend at the paper to go through the archive for the past twenty years, looking for any mention of severed ears and the Queensland Kings."

Zinnie looked up at him. "That must have taken a while! Isn't there a new paper every day?"

"Ah well, the *Scotsman* employs an archivist, you see, who goes through the new edition once it has been printed and cuts out several copies of every story. Then each is

157

carefully filed under a specific subject. That way, any journalist wanting to check what has been written about a subject previously can look through a vast store of what the paper has already published. Ingenious – and a vital tool for research. In this case, I told my friend to begin his efforts in the file for stories that took place in Queensland, Australia."

Zinnie tried to imagine what a room containing all those cut-up pieces of paper would look like. She hoped it was tidier that Conan Doyle's own desk.

"And this is what your friend found?" Zinnie asked, looking at the article in her hand.

"Quite so. Shall I read it to you?"

Zinnie handed back the paper with a brief nod and he began to read.

18th March 1867

THE SCOTSMAN

NOTORIOUS CRIMINALS TARGET NEW LOCOMOTIVE LINE

PASSENGERS INJURED DURING ATTACK

Queensland, Australia. The continued construction of the world's first narrow-gauge mainline railway is in question following a violent robbery.

At around 5 a.m. on Thursday 17 July, the locomotive encountered an obstruction on a curve in the line three miles south of the current terminus at Bigge's Camp. The quick-thinking and skill of the driver, Mr Harry Pinker of Brisbane, Queensland, prevented a worse catastrophe, but two carriages suffered derailment. The thieves were apparently aware that this particular train was carrying capital and wages sufficient to sustain the continued construction of the line into the Little Liverpool range of mountains.

While the driver and the uninjured attempted to tend to the small number of passengers hurt in the accident, five men attacked on horseback, wearing scarves tied over their lower faces and wielding pistols and clubs. They demanded access to the money, which according to unconfirmed reports was in excess of £20,000.

It was at this point that Mr Carlson Hobart, officer of Her Majesty's police force out of Brisbane, made himself known. He had been travelling out of uniform and at the behest of the Moreton Bay Tramway Company and was accompanied by his wife, Mrs Elsie Hobart. The officer behaved valiantly, attempting to fight off the attackers, but he was subdued by a blow to the head. While he was incapacitated, one of his ears was severed and removed from the scene, along with the money.

Eyewitnesses report that following the attack the thieves made off in the direction of the mountain range. They have not yet been caught. Though they disguised their identity, local sources have suggested this to be the boldest outrage by far of the Queensland Kings, a notorious gang of young ruffians who have taken advantage of the new state's remote aspect to rob and extort at will. Mr Hobart's terrible mutilation would also suggest this: the gang is previously known to have hacked off the ears of those who have attempted to stand in their way. The case is ongoing.

"None of the rest of the piece is relevant to our enquiry," said Conan Doyle, looking up. "What is relevant is that, two weeks later, four of the five men were captured, convicted and incarcerated. The fifth man was never found."

Zinnie took the piece of paper back and stared at the image of the stricken train. "Do you think MacDuff could be that last man? The one that got away?"

Conan Doyle sighed. "It's all just conjecture at this point. We have no proof that there's anything at all remiss with Mr Phineas MacDuff. And yet ... call it a hunch, Miss Zinnie, but yes – I do indeed believe he could be."

"Then ... the men who have died and had their ears lopped off are three of the other men who took part in the robbery?"

"That would make sense, wouldn't it?" Conan Doyle said.

"But what about the fourth man? Could he be the one killing the others?"

Conan Doyle spread his hands. "Well. Someone has been severing the ears of the Queensland Kings. Someone who knew – intimately, it would seem – their very precise method of exacting revenge. He has to be a firm suspect, doesn't he?"

"But why?" Zinnie asked. "If it was used as a punishment, why do that to members of your own gang?"

Conan Doyle shook his head. "Now that I don't know."

Zinnie got up and went to the desk, opening Conan

Doyle's notebook and flipping over to his sketches of the bodies. In death, the three men were all unkempt, yet she got the impression that they wouldn't have looked much different in life.

"They were all poor," she said, thinking out loud. "You thought they'd probably been sailors, come in on a ship, and they died in the gutter."

Conan Doyle nodded. "That's right."

"MacDuff isn't poor, though," she said. "He's very, very rich. You said all but one of the Queensland Kings were caught – do you know if the police ever recovered the stolen money?"

Conan Doyle stared up at her for a moment and then slapped his hand against his thigh. "They never did! The Moreton Bay Tramway Company folded a year later, dogged by the loss. By Jove, you've got it! Phineas MacDuff's fortune may well have come from that robbery."

Zinnie nodded. "By the time the rest of the Queensland Kings got out of jail, he was long gone, with the cash that had put them all behind bars. Maybe he never expected the gang to be freed. Maybe he thought he'd changed himself enough that he could never be recognized. But then they found him."

Conan Doyle looked down at the sketches. "But why would one kill the other three?"

Zinnie shrugged. "Perhaps they all tracked him down together but one of them decided he didn't need the others once they had. They're obviously ruthless enough to do something that terrible. That last man sent the ears to act as a warning to MacDuff that the past has finally caught up with him."

"Yes, yes, yes," whispered Conan Doyle. "I really think you've got it, Miss Zinnie. But knowing a thing is very different to proving it."

"Maybe we don't have to prove it," Zinnie said. "Maybe we just have to get him to confess to it."

"Confess?" Conan Doyle asked, mystified. "How on earth would we do that?"

"By holding a seance," Zinnie said. "In Mary King's Close."

CHAPTER 24

"I beg your pardon?" Conan Doyle said, with a look of utter astonishment on his face.

"Remember the seance at Lady Sarah's?" Zinnie pressed. "MacDuff kept going on about the Kings. He'd already had two pairs of ears sent to him by that point. He was planning to ask who was sending them to him."

"But he didn't get an answer," Conan Doyle pointed out. "The spirits wouldn't come to him."

Zinnie almost blurted out that of course they didn't because the whole stupid seance was a fake, but she stopped herself just in time.

"But, because of that, he doesn't know that the ears actually came from the Kings themselves, does he?" she pointed out instead. "So he must still be wondering who they belong to. The last seance didn't give him the answers

164

he wanted. But if we stage another one, he can ask again, can't he? He's had other ears arrive since then, so he must be beside himself by now. If he's desperate enough, he'll say something that we can use, I know it. He'll give something of himself away, something that will let us find the last man and get MacDuff arrested too."

"But why Mary King's Close?" Conan Doyle argued. "Surely it would be better to ask Lady Sarah if—"

"Because the ghost is back," Zinnie said, thinking quickly. "The one you and I heard. It's back. So we can kill two birds with one stone and find out why it's haunting the close at the same time."

Conan Doyle frowned. "But you were adamant it wasn't a ghost. You said—"

"Well, I've changed my mind," Zinnie said hurriedly. "I've heard it again. Seen it too. And so have Lady Sarah and Doctor Jex-Blake. Lady Sarah wants to find out why the spirit is restless, so I know she'll come to the seance, and that will persuade others to as well – including MacDuff."

Conan Doyle narrowed his eyes suspiciously. "You're up to something, Miss Zinnie. What is it?"

"Nothing," she said. "I just want to solve the mystery of the severed ears, that's all. And maybe put MacDuff behind bars, if it turns out we're right."

Conan Doyle said nothing but continued to watch her with a shrewd look. "My butler, Rawton, brought me a poster he'd found in the street the other day. He was adamant that the person on it looked like you. But it was a boy wanted for the theft of a pocket watch and so I told him he was mistaken. I've always trusted you and your sisters, Miss Zinnie. More than others have told me is wise. I'm not wrong to do so, am I?"

Zinnie set her jaw even as her stomach flipped unhappily. "No."

Conan Doyle nodded and thought for another moment. "Very well. I must admit, the idea of entreating the spirits in such a place as that underground maze is an intriguing one. Who knows what we'll call into our realm from beyond the veil."

"Great," Zinnie said, relieved. "Then will you tell Lady Sarah and MacDuff too? It'll be on Friday. Eleven o'clock, Mary King's Close. I'll ask the doctor."

"This Friday?" Conan Doyle asked, surprised again. "That's the day after tomorrow. Why such a rush?"

Zinnie shrugged. "No time like the present, is there? Anyway, if we don't move quickly, the last man might catch up with MacDuff before we do."

Conan Doyle eyed her again and she had an uncanny feeling that he could see right through her, as if she were nothing more than a spirit herself. Still, he nodded. "All right. We'll have to hope that neither the attendees nor the medium are already booked. It's very short notice."

"Don't worry about the medium," Zinnie said. "I'll deal with her. You just make sure the rest are there."

Zinnie's next stop after Picardy Place was the clinic to see Nell and Sadie. The sun was setting as she hurried across Waverley Bridge, the evening rain weighing down the slate-grey sky until it touched the castle's dark turrets. She kept an eye out for police as she neared the clinic, but there was no sign of a patrol and, besides, she doubted a passing lawman would give her so much as a second glance. She looked of as little note as every other poor woman she passed and just as invisible.

Mrs Collins opened the door to 73 Grove Street, pausing to look Zinnie up and down with her usual expression of slight disgust before letting her in.

"I'm not staying long," Zinnie said. "I just want to see my sisters."

The matron didn't respond but walked with Zinnie to the door of Nell's sickroom, as if convinced that she'd take off somewhere else in the house given half a chance. Zinnie wondered if she followed Sadie about in the same fashion. She could imagine Sadie putting up with it, but there's no way that Zinnie would. Bitter old bat! What would the Mrs Collinses of the world have to say about the doctor's idea of Sadie training alongside her? Zinnie almost laughed out loud. It'd be worth it just to see the look on the sour old goat's face.

"Zinnie!"

It was Nell's voice that greeted her – weak and hoarse but there. The little girl was lying propped up in a cloud of pillows with Sadie at her side.

"Nell!" Zinnie ran to the bed and scooped her into a hug, horribly aware of how thin her sister was. "You're awake!"

"She's doing well," Sadie said with a tired smile. "We were worried for a bit but now it looks as if she's really on the mend."

"The doctor and Sadie say I can't get out of bed yet," Nell said, her voice muffled against Zinnie's neck. "But soon I'll be up and about and then we can all go home. Can't we?"

Zinnie glanced at Sadie over Nell's head. Sadie looked away, smoothing the rumpled blanket instead of meeting her eye.

"Just you keep getting better, pippin. Don't think of anything else yet," Zinnie said, settling the girl back against her pillows and tucking her in before kissing her forehead. It was cooler now, without that horrible heat running beneath the skin. "Now I'm going to talk to Sadie for a little while, all right?" She watched as Nell nodded sleepily.

"Zinnie—" Sadie began as the two sisters went out into the corridor. She hesitated, stopping herself.

"What?" Zinnie asked. "What is it?"

Sadie hesitated and then nodded towards the door of Nell's room. "Do you really think we can go back to the way we've been living? We nearly lost Nell. She's still not as strong as she was, and she won't be for a long time. If she goes back to living in the same way, she's going to get sick again. Maybe next time we won't be so lucky."

"Then what are you saying?" Zinnie asked. "That you want her to go to an orphanage?"

"Would that really be so bad?" Sadie asked. "She'd be in a clean, safe place."

"Safe!" Zinnie repeated. She stared at her sister. "She wouldn't be safe! You know what it was like for me there! Do you really want Nell to go through the same?"

Sadie winced and looked away. Zinnie rarely spoke about how she'd grown up. She'd never known her ma or her pa – she'd been just a baby when she'd been left on the steps of a 'school' that said it took care of children with nowhere else to go. It was supposed to be a good place, a safe place, but all the owners were interested in was raising girls until they were old enough to be sent to homes that wanted servants. Even when a girl found a place to take her, she didn't escape the orphanage because it was then that the owners started to take payment for her 'care'. Her wages were never her own. They always went back to the 'home'. It was in that place that Zinnie had learned to do without much to eat, to sleep on hard surfaces in cold, damp rooms. It was there she promised herself that she would never owe anyone anything, and that adults were not to be trusted.

"I know you had a terrible time," her sister said quietly. "But Doctor Jex-Blake promises that we can find a good place for her – a decent place with people who care. I could stay here, to train, and you can go to Lady Sarah's. We won't have to go back to the closes, ever."

"But we'd be apart," Zinnie said. "Is that really what you want?"

"Of course it isn't, but it wouldn't be forever. If we're both working, we can save, can't we? We could find enough to rent a place – a proper place – together. And then we can bring Nell home to that. It'd be a real home, Zinnie, clean and warm."

"Even if all that really were a thing we could hope for," Zinnie said, "you're forgetting one thing. What about Aelfine? We can't just leave her on her own."

Sadie twined her fingers together, not looking Zinnie in the eye. "There are places she could go. Places that would know how to look after her properly."

Zinnie recoiled. "You mean … an asylum?"

"They're not bad places, Zinnie," Sadie said desperately. "I found a book about them, in the doctor's library."

"They're for mad people, Sadie! People who can't look after themselves, people who need to be locked up all day, every day! Aelfine ran away because she didn't want to be in a cage – how can we even think about letting anyone put her back in one? She's not mad or stupid. She's just different, that's all. Can't you see that?"

"Of course I can! But we can't help everyone, Zinnie. Look at us! We can't even help ourselves. With Talbot and

MacDuff looking for her, she'd be safer there, wouldn't she? And then we can … we can…"

"We can *what*?" Zinnie asked sharply.

Sadie looked at Zinnie with tears in her eyes. Then she hung her head, wisps of her unruly red hair – cleaner than Zinnie had ever seen it; she must have had a bath since she'd been in the clinic – slipped down to hide her face.

"Am I wrong?" Sadie asked, her words clogged with tears. "Am I wrong to want *this*, instead of what we've got?"

Zinnie's heart clenched. They were standing in a whitewashed hallway so clean she could still smell the vinegar with which it had been scrubbed. Sadie would sleep that night in a bed set beside their little sister's, something they had only done once before, when Zinnie had saved up enough for them all to rent a single hostel bed to share in Grassmarket. That had felt like they'd fallen into riches, even though it had been little more than straw on a pallet and they were as crammed in together as they were in Mary King's Close.

Here, in the doctor's clinic, they'd get up and wash with clean water, dress in clean clothes and eat a breakfast that wasn't too rotten to sell to richer people. Sadie had been given a chance to have that every day: she'd been given a chance at a future that few girls like them ever even dreamed of, it was so unlikely. How could Zinnie begrudge her that?

She pulled Sadie into a hug. "Of course you aren't,"

Zinnie said, resting her chin on her sister's head. "I've just got to find a way to keep everyone safe, Aelfine as well. But I know how to do that now."

Sadie pulled back and looked up at Zinnie with a tear-stained face. "What do you mean?"

CHAPTER 25

By the time Zinnie was making her way back towards the Old Town, it was dark and the rain was lashing out of the sky in wind-blown torrents. Cold and wet, she went first to Writers' Court.

Constance McQuirter had a smoking fire burning in her dirty grate, the wind and rain battering in through the rotten gaps around her windowpane.

"Well, well," she said, pulling open the door no more than a crack. "Look what not even the cat would drag in. Be off with you – you've got all the help you're going to get from me."

"Help?" Zinnie repeated, as rainwater dripped from her hair and ran down her nose. "That wasn't help, Constance, that was just repayment. *Now* you're going to help me." She put her foot in the open doorway before Constance could push it shut. "Or have you forgotten what I know?"

"Two can play at that game," the woman warned her. "I've seen your pinched little face on posters, so I have. All it takes is a word in the right copper's ear and off you'll go, ragamuffin thief."

Zinnie tried another tack. She removed her foot and turned to leave. "All right, all right. Look, all I wanted was to put some money your way. Figured it might as well come to you as old Mother Goodwynd. But if you're not interested…"

The door opened quickly. "Hold on. Mother Goodwynd? What would you want with that old trollop?"

"For the seance, of course."

"What seance?"

"The one Lady Sarah wants to hold down in Mary King's Close. She's got a mind to find out who the ghost is haunting down there. You heard that it's back?"

"Lady Sarah?" Constance said, paling. "But she's one of my regulars!"

"Aye, I know," said Zinnie, making as if to turn away. "That's why she told me to ask you first. But you said no, so—"

"Wait! That was before I knew what it was all about," Constance said, grabbing her arm and pulling Zinnie back round to face her. "Of course I'll do it for Lady Sarah."

Zinnie smiled. "That's good then. This Friday, ten o'clock sharp. All right? Everyone else will be arriving at eleven."

"This Friday?" Constance repeated. "But that's—"

"No bother if you can't," Zinnie said chirpily. "It's short notice, I know. I'll just go and knock on Mother Goodwynd's door—"

"No," Constance said, through gritted teeth. "This Friday it is. Ten o'clock."

Zinnie grinned. "Her ladyship will be pleased."

Constance gave her a look that was as laced with suspicion as Conan Doyle's had been. "Are you up to something? You going to lure a punnet of fine folk down there and then rob them blind?"

"Oh, I'd never dream of that," Zinnie said, heading for the stairs. "I'll leave the robbery to you, Constance. You're an old hand at it, after all."

Outside, the night sky was still spearing the earth with rain. There were no stars to be seen at all. The alley had been swallowed by shadows, thick and dark. If not for the echo, Zinnie would have walked straight into the path of the men coming her way. As it was, she recognized the harsh brag of Bartholomew Talbot's voice. She ducked back into Writers' Court with barely a second to spare as he and his men barrelled past, talking loudly, the potential for violence in every move they made. Her heart pounded in her chest, the healing bruises on her throat ached with remembered pain and Zinnie hated, hated, *hated* it, the hold the fear of him had over her.

She waited a moment or two, until they had vanished

into the broken underworld of Mary King's Close. Then she slipped back out into the alley, very nearly colliding with the dark silhouette of a figure that stood head and shoulders over her. She leaped back with a short cry.

"Watch it," growled a quiet voice, as the moon sparked from behind the monotonous grey cloud just long enough for her to see the outline of a man. He had a wide-brimmed hat pulled low over one ear, the gleam of a gold ring in the other and an angry glint in his dark eyes.

The moon slipped away again and the figure went on, quickly swallowed by shadows. She couldn't tell whether he'd gone down into the close or continued on. Had he been following Talbot?

Zinnie left enough time to be sure of a good distance between her and Talbot's men. She kept her eyes peeled as she made for the close and then down its rain-slicked flags to where Aelfine and Ruby were hidden.

She waited in the darkness of the ruined room for a few minutes before giving the whistle they had agreed on. A little longer still and Zinnie heard a soft scuffling sound. Then there were Aelfine and Ruby, standing in front of her.

"All right?" she whispered. Aelfine nodded. "Good. It's time for you to show me everything. OK?"

Aelfine and Ruby shared a brief look, and then Aelfine reached out and took the candle stub from Zinnie and blew it out. She gripped Zinnie's hand and silently began to lead her towards the abyss that dominated the room.

Zinnie's stomach turned over, her heart beginning to race. She'd tried and tried to find a way round the hole. She'd never made it, not once.

"Don't worry," said Aelfine's voice, so quietly that it was barely there. "Ruby will help you. You have to trust us."

Ruby gave a tiny chitter that came from somewhere near Zinnie's left foot. A second later, she felt tiny paws against her ankle and faint pressure as the monkey pushed her foot in a particular direction.

"Just do as Ruby tells you," Aelfine said, and then let go of Zinnie's hand. Zinnie almost flailed, convinced she was going to fall into the void below, but Ruby pushed at her foot again and, when she moved it, Zinnie felt those little hands pulling and then pressing down. Zinnie took the step, and her foot landed on something solid in the darkness. She wobbled, but a second later Ruby's paws were against her other foot, guiding it in the same way. Zinnie stretched out her arms, feeling for something to grip. The fingers of her left hand brushed against the wall, dislodging dust and flakes of brick.

Zinnie knew that, although the floor had almost completely gone, there were still remnants of broken floorboards jutting out over the hole. When she'd tried to get round the void before, she'd always been too afraid to risk putting all her weight on one after the other, because if one broke there would be no way to stop herself falling. But it was clear that Aelfine and Ruby had worked out which ones were still strong enough to bear a person's weight. These were what Ruby was guiding her feet towards, one by one. Zinnie gave in to the idea that all she had to do was move exactly when and where the monkey told her to, and everything would be fine. After all, what else could she do?

Step by agonizing step, Zinnie let herself be drawn across the void. Sometimes she reached out her questing fingers to brush against the wall, which at least gave her an idea that there was something solid around her somewhere. The bells of St Giles clanged, as distant from Mary King's Close as the moon itself. Midnight it was, and as dark as Zinnie had ever known.

CHAPTER 26

Beyond the broken floor was a space that might once have had a door fitted to it, but now stood open like a missing tooth. Inside was another small room, just as ruined as every other in Mary King's Close. The ceiling here had fallen in too, but the floor, though littered with debris, seemed to be sound. Aelfine didn't stop, instead leading Zinnie to the left, into another room without a door.

"Mind," Aelfine warned, and Zinnie looked down to see many candle stubs on the floor, standing upright amid more rubble.

"Where did all these come from?" Zinnie asked, as she stepped over them. She could just make out Aelfine's shrug in the gloom.

"Ruby got them," she said.

"Right," Zinnie said, imagining the little creature with

armfuls of pilfered candles. "Useful."

Aelfine picked one up and lit it. The light revealed, pushed against the wall, the pile of blankets that they had taken from their corner, along with a half-eaten loaf of bread and a pitcher of milk – Ruby again, Zinnie surmised, although how the little monkey had managed to carry the milk across that void was anyone's guess. As Zinnie looked around, something caught her eye. It flickered in the dark room they had passed through first – a dancing flame, floating in mid-air. She jumped.

"Cripes!" she said. "What's that? Who's there?"

Aelfine laughed and blew out the candle she held. The one in the other room vanished too.

"What – how did you do that?" Zinnie asked, mystified.

Aelfine led her back across the floor to the doorway of the room and lit the candle again, holding it out beneath Zinnie's chin. This time Zinnie was shocked to see a version of her own face looking back at her, shadows pooling round her eyes and under her nose. Aelfine pulled the candle back towards her own face and a mirror image of it flickered before them, disembodied and strange, for all the world a ghost from beyond the veil.

"Come see," Aelfine said, and walked back into the first room, still holding her candle in her outstretched hand.

The other candle flame grew larger as Aelfine got closer to it, the rest of her head and shoulders coming into view too, until she stopped, reached out and tapped the candle she held to the one in front of her. They met with a tiny knocking sound, and Zinnie realized that she was looking at a glass panel that was standing at an angle, just inside the empty doorway. Now that she knew what to look for, she could see the edges of the oblong pane.

"A reflection!" she said, amazed. "It's just a reflection!"

"That's how we make the ghost," Aelfine said, as if she were simply saying, 'Here is my handkerchief.' "And then Ruby goes up and –" she gestured with her hand to the crumbling walls – "makes noises."

Zinnie went to the pane of glass. It had been propped up between pieces of the broken ceiling and was all but invisible in the heavy darkness of the room. It looked like the panels she had seen stacked up in MacDuff's House of Wonders, waiting to be fitted into one of his cabinets.

"Where did you get the glass?" she asked.

Aelfine looked away and bit her lip. "Borrowed it."

"From MacDuff?"

Aelfine nodded, a guilty look on her face.

"It's all right," Zinnie said. "I don't care that you took it. But – how the devil did you get it all the way from George Street? And then down here, across that floor over there?"

Aelfine shrugged. "It was very dark. I borrowed a barrow. I had my cloak. And Ruby helped."

"But—"

"I took the barrow back," Aelfine said defensively. "I didn't steal. Only borrowed."

"Well," Zinnie said, still flummoxed, "that's good. But … how did you get it over that hole out there?"

"There's another way in." Aelfine turned and pointed up to the broken ceiling.

"Another…" Zinnie gaped at her. "Then why on earth did you make me climb over that hellhole to get here?"

"You wanted us to show you exactly how we did it!"

"OK," Zinnie said. "I suppose I asked for that." She was still trying to take in the fact that Aelfine had managed to come up with this plan and put it into motion with only one small monkey to help her. And she'd all but cleared out Mary King's Close in the process. "Tell me again how you learned to do this. It was at the circus, you said?"

Aelfine nodded. "There was a magician. He had his own tent, with a stage. The Magnificent Marko. I wasn't supposed to go in there but I did. I hid. I watched."

Zinnie shook her head, still amazed. "Did your mother know that you could do this? Did MacDuff?"

A shadow settled in Aelfine's eyes at the mention of MacDuff's name. "I never told him anything. He's a bad man."

Zinnie placed a hand on the girl's shoulder and squeezed. "I know he is. But we're going to make him pay, Aelfine. I promise. We're going to hold a seance right here, where everyone will be able to see your ghost. And the ghost is going to tell everyone where to find your mother, all right? You do remember, don't you? You remember where he hid her … after … he did what he did?"

Tears filled Aelfine's eyes and she squeezed them shut, sobbing in a breath.

"I'm sorry," Zinnie said softly. "I know it's horrible. But in a little while I'll need you to tell me exactly how to find her. I have to know everything to make this work. When it's done, I promise you and Ruby will be safe from MacDuff. Forever."

Ruby began to babble. At first Zinnie thought the monkey was just agreeing with her but then the cries grew more frantic, sharp little yips of warning as the monkey stood by the door to the main room, looking out over the void.

"Someone's out there," Aelfine said. "Someone's coming."

Zinnie was instantly on alert. "Shh, Ruby," she hushed, straining to listen through the darkness. Footsteps echoed in the distance – at least two pairs, heavy and lumbering, and with them came voices, moving closer. "Aelfine, blow out the candle!"

Aelfine did as she was told and the three of them sat in darkness, straining to hear.

"Thought I heard something," said one of the voices, muffled by distance. "Down here it was."

"There's naught down here," said another. "Naught but the unnatural spirit. The ghost."

"There's no ghost," scoffed the first voice, and Zinnie

felt a jolt of fear as she recognized it. *Talbot!* "Just a bunch of lackwits yakking to each other."

"I've heard it with my very own earholes," said the first voice. "Screeching like the devil it was, like something straight out of hell. There's nothing in this life that can make a sound like that."

"Is that right?" Talbot drawled, louder now, growing ever nearer. "You've heard every strange creature that walks this earth, have you, Galbraith? You've been to every country and catalogued them all in that tiny mind of yours, like a scholar?"

Zinnie held her breath as the footsteps reached the room without a floor.

"There's not a thing alive that could make a living down here, boss," said Galbraith. "I say let's go back."

"Just you wait a minute," said Talbot, his voice low, calm and dangerous in a way that made Zinnie's skin crawl and her heart leap into her throat. "You're not afraid, are you? Big, strong feller like you? You ain't afraid of the dark?"

"Course not."

"You won't mind going a little deeper then, will you? Wonder what's on the other side of that nasty hole. Never been this far down before. Always did have a taste for new things, me…"

Ruby, who had been sitting huddled beside Aelfine, suddenly became a blur of movement. She leaped up and skittered across the floor on all fours, disappearing out of the empty doorway before either Aelfine or Zinnie could react. A split second later, the haunting screech that had so terrified the inhabitants of the closes echoed down from above.

"Oh no," Zinnie whispered. "Ruby, no. Not now!"

"She's scaring them off," Aelfine whispered. "That's all. They'll think it's the ghost. They'll go away."

"They won't," Zinnie said. "Not this time. Talbot won't." Even as she said it, Zinnie realized how true her words were. Talbot was as evil as MacDuff. He was also fearless and very, very clever. That's what made him so dangerous. MacDuff was paying him to look for two things – a girl and a monkey. Talbot would have wanted to know everything about what the monkey looked and *sounded* like. And when he'd heard tell of strange noises way down at the bottom of the close... That's why he was down here. It had to be.

Ruby's screech came again.

"Can you tell her to stop?" Zinnie whispered, panicked. "Without shouting? Is there a signal—"

Aelfine raised her fingers to her lips and whistled through them, a short, piercing ring of sound that made Zinnie wince, for it would surely be as recognizable as a voice for anyone listening closely. Ruby's screech died instantly.

"That's it!" Galbraith was crying. "That's the ghost! This place is haunted, Talbot. I'm telling you! I'm off—"

185

There came the sound of running feet but Zinnie only counted one pair. She held her breath, clutching Aelfine's hand.

"Was it now?" came Talbot's thoughtful voice, from the darkness, and Zinnie's skin crawled anew. "So that's what one of them sounds like, is it? Well, I suppose now I know."

Then Ruby's cries began again. They began to move away, getting quieter as they moved up the close. The sound of her shrieks rose and dipped before rising again, as if she were ducking in and out of rooms. Zinnie strained to hear Talbot's movements. For long moments he seemed to be standing entirely still. Then there was the crunch of footsteps as he left the room and made his way back up Mary King's Close.

"He's going after Ruby!" Zinnie realized.

"Yes," Aelfine said proudly. "She's leading him away."

"But what if he catches her?"

"Don't worry," Aelfine whispered. "She's faster than he is. And she knows how to hide. Come on. I'll show you the other way out."

CHAPTER 27

"Where are they now?" Sadie asked the next morning, when Zinnie had gone to the clinic to tell her what had happened. "You didn't leave them there?"

"It's the safest place for them," Zinnie said. They were sitting in the corner of Nell's room while the little girl slumbered. "No one can get across that hole in the floor without Ruby and Aelfine to guide them."

Sadie shivered. "I bet Talbot could."

"Even if he did, Ruby would hear him coming, which gives them enough time to escape. Don't worry," Zinnie said with more confidence than she felt. "MacDuff will be behind bars soon enough."

"You can't mean to go ahead with the seance?" Sadie said, horrified. "You can't, not now. Talbot will tell MacDuff that he suspects Aelfine and Ruby are down there and

MacDuff will realize it's all a trick!"

"It doesn't matter."

"What do you mean?" Sadie cried, her voice rising. "How could it possibly not matter? He's a murderer, Zinnie, and you know what Talbot's like. They're both too dangerous to play games with!"

"I don't have a choice," Zinnie said. "We can't go to the police and, even if we could, no one's going to take our word over MacDuff's. The seance will expose him for what he is, Sadie, in a way that no one can argue with. The ghost will tell them where to find the body. Then he'll be finished."

"You think that will be enough? Finding the body?"

A sudden finger of doubt probed Zinnie's heart. "Why wouldn't it be?"

"What if it still doesn't prove what happened?" Sadie asked, biting her lip. "Zinnie, if this doesn't work, we're all going to be in terrible trouble."

"Who's in terrible trouble?"

The voice came from the doorway behind them. It was Doctor Jex-Blake, standing there with a slight smile on her face and both eyebrows raised in question.

"No one now," Zinnie said, as quick as a flash, with a bright smile. "But Nell would have been if we hadn't had you to help us. Thank you, Doctor."

Jex-Blake entered the room, still smiling. "It was my pleasure. Anyway, Sadie has done a lot of the work. She really is a natural, you know."

Zinnie glanced at her sister, who was looking at her toes with an embarrassed smile. "Nell won't need to be here much longer, will she?"

The doctor smiled again. "I hope not, although there's no rush for her to leave. The clinic beds are quiet at present and she's such a sweet child to have around. Besides, we still have things to discuss about her future. Don't we?"

Zinnie ignored the tremor in her heart. "Let's leave it until after tomorrow," she said. "Then we'll talk about it. All right?"

"After tomorrow?" the doctor repeated. "Do you mean this seance that's being held in Mary King's Close? I must confess, it sounds very strange to me, although Lady Sarah is all abuzz with excitement over it. You've got something to do with it, haven't you, Zinnie? Was it your idea?"

Zinnie shrugged. "You ladies seemed so keen to know why the ghost was there. Just made sense. That's all."

Doctor Jex-Blake gave her a shrewd look. "This isn't … something else that Arthur Conan Doyle has put you up to, for some purpose of his own, like that pocket watch that so nearly got you into trouble?"

"No, Doctor. It's nothing to do with Mr Conan Doyle." *That isn't a lie, either, is it?* Zinnie thought to herself. *Not really.*

"You're sure there's nothing else you want to tell me about it?"

Zinnie resisted the urge to look at Sadie. "Only that

you should come, Doctor. It might be … interesting … for you."

"Yes," the doctor said, in a tone of voice that made Zinnie a little nervous. "No doubt it will."

Sadie's words about the body stayed with Zinnie as she left the clinic and walked back towards home. The seance would be hard enough to manage as it was – if it ended badly, with MacDuff still at large and Aelfine still in danger, then all was lost. Zinnie thought hard as she made her way along Morrison Street, the morning early enough for the office clerks to still be making their way to their day's billets.

By the time she'd reached the crossing of Lothian Road, she'd decided what she must do. She had to go back to the House of Wonders and find something that would prove beyond all doubt that it was MacDuff who had murdered Aelfine's mother. It was risky and she would never be able to tell anyone what she had done, but if it meant making sure that MacDuff ended up behind bars, and that Aelfine and Ruby were safe from him, it would be worth it.

Going back to Mary King's Close, she picked up the bag that Lady Sarah's butler had given her the night of the seance and stuffed the maid's outfit that she had yet to return into it before slinging it over her shoulder. Then, checking around her to see that she wasn't being watched, she slipped back down to Aelfine's hiding place.

The alternative route that the girl and the monkey had shown her was difficult to find, especially from the other direction and without a guide. It involved scrambling up and over a partially collapsed wall and down on to a pile of rubble that looked as if it couldn't possibly lead anywhere. It took Zinnie some time to find her way, and she did it without the help of a candle for fear of drawing attention. It was slow-going, but she didn't mind – that meant it was unlikely Talbot would find his way here, not without someone showing him first. Besides, despite the danger, Zinnie just found it exciting to explore somewhere new.

When all this is over, she told herself, *I'm going see what other places like this are down here.* After all, maybe there was a better place for the sisters to establish a home.

"Aelfine," Zinnie called softly, once she'd made it into the hidden room. "It's me."

Aelfine made her jump by appearing out of the shadows as quietly as a cat. The two girls hugged.

"Are you all right?" Zinnie asked.

"Yes," said Aelfine. "No one has come since you left."

"Good. Now I need to ask you something. It's about your ma."

Aelfine nodded, biting her lip. Zinnie squeezed her hand.

"Can you think of something that she owned that no one else would have had?" Zinnie asked. "Something that, if you or anyone else saw it, you'd know it was hers straight away? A necklace maybe? Earrings? It needs to be small."

Aelfine looked away, a frown on her face as she thought. "Her ball," she said. "Only Ma has the ball."

For a moment Zinnie was confused. "A ball?"

Aelfine made a circle shape with both hands. "She used it to see things. To tell fortunes."

"Ah!" Zinnie suddenly saw what Aelfine meant. "A crystal ball! Of course!"

Aelfine nodded. "It's only little, but it cost a lot of money and she couldn't afford a bigger one. She said once it was the most expensive thing she owned. She always wrapped it in her shawls when she'd finished working. To keep it safe."

Zinnie's heart soared. "That's perfect. Thank you."

She went to move away again, and then had another thought and turned back. "And … what about MacDuff?"

Aelfine shrugged. "His hat?"

Zinnie chewed her lip, thinking. "I'll never get hold of that." She thought about when she'd first seen him, at the seance, dressed up in his finery, and snapped her fingers. "His handkerchiefs! He has his name embroidered on his handkerchiefs!"

Aelfine looked puzzled. Zinnie hugged her. "Don't worry," she said. "There's just something I need to do. I'll be back soon, all right?"

Once Zinnie had crept out of Mary King's Close again, she headed straight for George Street.

The House of Wonders was closed, its gaudy painted advertising still proclaiming what curiosities would soon be seen within. Zinnie made for the backstreet again, hoping that the rear entrance would be open as before, but it seemed her luck would not hold, not today. The double doors were bolted shut. She tried them carefully but the lock was unassailable, at least without a set of bolt cutters.

Zinnie looked for another way in, checking every now and then that none of the passing traffic was paying her any note. That was how she spotted him, standing in the shadows at the mouth of another alley opposite. A tall man with a wide-brimmed hat pulled down low on one side of his head. He was watching MacDuff's place. She ducked away from the door, hoping that the flurry of people passing between them had concealed her own interest. She moved a little way down the street, where she could still make him out without fear of being seen herself.

It was the man she'd bumped into in the dark in Writers' Court, Zinnie was sure of it – the one who had been following Talbot. It was the same hat pulled down in the same unusual way, the same glinting earring, the same stern eyes.

Zinnie crept a little closer, dodging between the discarded crates and boxes that lined the narrow alleyway. The man's gaze seemed fixed on MacDuff's place, as if he were waiting for something. Or someone.

He turned abruptly at the sound of a noise behind him,

and as he did so Zinnie saw exactly why his hat was at such an obscure angle.

He only had one ear.

For a split second she froze. Then she turned and fled. Zinnie ran all the way to Picardy Place and only stopped ringing the bell at Arthur Conan Doyle's house when his butler threw open the door with a disgruntled look on his face.

"I've found him," she gasped through the open door, her words meant for the figure descending the stairs behind his butler. "I've found the other Queensland King."

"But that is not possible," said Arthur Conan Doyle. "He's dead."

CHAPTER 28

"Look here, you see?" said Conan Doyle, opening his notebook and laying it flat on his desk, pointing to a new sketch. "The cadaver arrived at the hospital just yesterday afternoon, found in the Leith below Warriston Cemetery. Rawton," he said to the butler, as Zinnie bent over the sketch. "Bring us both coffee, would you? Quick as you can."

The picture Conan Doyle had drawn showed the head, torso and upper arms of a large, thick-necked man with short dark hair and lips that seemed to be twisted into a permanent sneer. An old scar ran down one cheek, starting so close to his right eye that Zinnie thought he'd probably been lucky not to lose it. More notable, though, was the lack of both his ears and the burn marks that curved over his chest, as if he had been trying to remove a large tattoo once inked there.

"He looks very much like our first three unfortunates, does he not?" said Conan Doyle.

"Yes," Zinnie said. "But if he was the fourth man, and MacDuff is the fifth, then who's the man with only one ear I just saw? He can't be part of the gang – he must be someone else. And why would anyone else be sending MacDuff the ears of his old friends?"

"Perhaps we have this backwards," Conan Doyle said carefully. "Perhaps MacDuff is as much a victim here as a criminal, after all."

"No!" Zinnie snapped. "He's a murderer, I know it. He killed the fortune-teller and he'll kill again to stop anyone finding out about it if he has the chance!"

"The fortune-teller?" Conan Doyle was looking at Zinnie with interest. "You've mentioned this before. I thought the woman had just left his company."

"No. He killed her, and if he can find her he'll kill…" Zinnie pulled herself up just in time, but Conan Doyle still noticed.

"He'll kill whom?" he said, his face taking on a look of concern. "Miss Zinnie, what's going on? What haven't you told me?"

Rawton chose that moment to arrive with the coffee, which gave Zinnie time to collect her thoughts.

"Listen to me," Conan Doyle said, once the butler had gone again. "If you have evidence that MacDuff has done something terrible, or is planning to do so, then we must go to the police at once."

"I don't," Zinnie said. "But I will. After the seance."

"The seance?" he repeated, puzzled. "What do you mean? What are you planning, Miss Zinnie? I must know!"

"I can't tell you," Zinnie said, wishing she'd never come here this morning. Part of her wanted to tell Conan Doyle about Aelfine, about all of it. But she'd promised not to give her new sister up to the doctors of whom she was so terrified. And besides they were just one more day away from everything falling into place without Zinnie needing to break her confidence.

"You just have to trust me. Everything will be fine after the seance."

"Miss Zinnie—"

"*Don't*," she said. "Don't ask me. I promised."

Conan Doyle frowned at her. "But it has to do with MacDuff and all will be revealed at the seance?" At Zinnie's nod, he sighed heavily. "Oh, Miss Zinnie. What have you got yourself into?"

"It'll be worth it," Zinnie said, trying to convince herself as much as him. "It's all going to be fine."

He watched her for another moment and then nodded. "If your mind is made up, then I suppose there's not much I can do, is there?"

"No," said Zinnie. Then she was hit by a brainwave so blindingly brilliant she almost dropped her coffee cup. "Yes! I need Lady Sarah's help. Her butler will shut the door in my face if I go there alone, but not if you're there."

Conan Doyle made a face, sipped his coffee and then rang for the butler again to ask for his carriage.

"More subterfuge? How perfectly wonderful!" exclaimed Lady Sarah. Today the scarlet bird was perched directly on her shoulder. The brilliant red of its feathers contrasted starkly with the yellow satin of the dress Lady Sarah wore as it rubbed its great beak against her cheek and watched the room with a beady eye. Zinnie tried to imagine this grand lady hacking her way through a jungle but just couldn't.

"You know, I've been wondering about that man MacDuff myself. He was so very bullish at the seance. And I've been dying to look round the House of Wonders, but alas it's still not open."

"I doubt he will refuse you, my lady," said Conan Doyle.

"Say you're leaving town and you wanted to see it before you left, so you can tell all your friends whether they should make the effort to go themselves," Zinnie suggested. "That should do the trick."

"Still, it would be uncouth to simply turn up on his doorstep entirely unannounced," said Lady Sarah. "He might be out."

"Even better," said Zinnie. "None of his lackeys would turn away Lady Sarah Montague – and her maid – now, would they?" Zinnie held up the bag she'd brought. It still contained the uniform she'd borrowed the night of the seance.

Lady Sarah considered this and then looked at Conan Doyle. "Can we use your carriage, Arthur, since it's here already?"

"Of course, Lady Sarah."

"You know what this is about, I suppose?"

"Actually, my lady, I am as much in the dark as you are."

Lady Sarah's eyes twinkled. "Indeed? Well, it's about time someone played Arthur at his own game. Is he to accompany us on this outing, Zinnie?"

"That's a good idea," Zinnie said. "Lady Sarah can keep MacDuff occupied and Mr Conan Doyle can keep an eye open while I do what I need to do."

A flicker of doubt danced across Lady Sarah's face. "I realize I am about to willingly aid a criminal activity. You can assure me this is for the very best of reasons?"

"The very best," Zinnie said. "You'll see that soon. I promise."

CHAPTER 29

Their luck, it turned out, was at its best. MacDuff was not in, attending to some matter elsewhere in the town. Conan Doyle got out to knock, leaving Lady Sarah and Zinnie in the carriage at the kerb. One glimpse of her ladyship in all her finery had sent the clerk who opened the door into a fluster.

"What a very great pity," Lady Sarah called, leaning through the carriage window, the plumes of her ostrich-feather hat fluttering lightly in the breeze. "I leave town on Sunday and will be gone for some months. I was hoping to see the exhibits before I went."

"Well," said the clerk nervously, "I am sorry, my lady, but—"

"We know, of course," added Conan Doyle, "that Mr MacDuff, having himself been a guest at Montague House, would be loath to think that he had turned away Lady Sarah, who has so very many friends among the sort of people he would love to have as visitors here."

The clerk's face went pale. "Well, I mean – that is to say, sir, I'm sure Mr MacDuff would not dream of turning Lady Sarah away were he here himself to receive her."

Conan Doyle raised his eyebrows. "But is there no one within that he trusts to conduct a tour in his stead? Dear oh dear, that sounds rather worrying."

"Not at all, sir. I am very knowledgeable about each exhibit and trusted by Mr MacDuff himself, but—"

"Excellent!" Conan Doyle exclaimed, turning back to the carriage, flicking open the door and holding out his hand. "Marvellous! Then that's the answer. My lady, if you please…"

Before the clerk knew it, Lady Sarah Montague, her full height over seven feet when feathers, boots and all were accounted for, was standing on the doorstep of the House of Wonders, her dress gleaming like gold beneath her travelling cloak. What could he do but welcome her in? Zinnie slipped in behind them, so plain in her borrowed maid's outfit that her presence was entirely eclipsed by Lady Sarah's customary ostentation. The clerk didn't even notice she was there, so preoccupied was he with his other two guests.

"Now," said Lady Sarah, once inside, "let's see what you have, my man."

"Not everything is finished, my lady. Some of the exhibits—"

"Never mind that. I shall make allowances, of course." She strode ahead, leading the clerk into the semi-darkness of the rooms. "Ah, what an impressive array of weaponry. Do you have curare darts and blowpipes from the jungle regions of South America? I have always been curious to see them. Such an ingenious method of dispatching one's enemies."

Zinnie hung back, letting the party draw ahead of her. The lower level and entrance to the house were laid out in much the same way as the floor above that she had already seen. A ticket booth stood to one side and beyond it a series of interconnected rooms full of cabinets. To her left, behind the booth, was a curved staircase, a rope across it closing it off to visitors. She waited until the other three had turned their attention to the first cabinet, the clerk's voice stuttering nervously as he launched into an explanation of its contents. Then, in the space of a heartbeat, Zinnie was under the rope and up the stairs.

They led her to the other end of the floor she'd already seen once. Directly ahead was the room where Aelfine and Ruby had been destined to spend their days. Zinnie's feet were silent on the floor as she headed not for the cage itself, but for the fortune-teller's tent.

But it was no longer there.

The dismay of this discovery brought Zinnie to a shocked

standstill. The room now contained nothing but Aelfine's enclosure, empty and dark but still ominous. Zinnie turned round, as if she might have somehow been disoriented by her arrival up different stairs, and saw a pile of objects in one corner. In the dim light, it took her a moment to realize that it was actually the tent – it had been dismantled ready for removal, proof that MacDuff knew for sure that the fortune-teller would not return.

Zinnie hurried over to the pile and was relieved to find the trunk she'd seen on her first visit half buried beneath woven rugs. She shoved them from its top and fumbled open the lid. Within was the same pile of dresses. Zinnie pulled one out and then plunged her hands to the very bottom of the trunk, searching for the fortune-teller's trinket. She knew she had minutes at most – she couldn't risk being caught. Then her fingers brushed something round and hard and she grabbed at the object, drawing it out. The crystal ball shone strangely in the weak light.

Zinnie pulled out a headscarf too and closed the trunk, wrapping the crystal ball in the scarf and then in one of the dresses as she gathered it up. She pushed this bundle into the bag that had previously carried the maid's outfit and slung it over her shoulder. Then she made for the door she had used to enter the first time she had sneaked in.

Once through it, she could hear banging and hammering from the second floor. The rest of the house seemed to be quiet. In front of her were the stairs that led down to the ground floor, while the main staircase continued up to her left. To her right there was a corridor that obviously ran behind the rear wall of the exhibition rooms, with doors to rooms on its left side. This wasn't as richly decorated as the exhibition rooms themselves and was obviously meant only for those who worked at the house, not visitors – exactly what Zinnie was looking for.

She slipped along the corridor, checking behind her to be sure that no one was coming. She listened at each door she came to, mindful that there might be people working within, but could hear nothing. Then she arrived at a door that bore a brass plate with what was probably a name engraved upon it. *Who else*, Zinnie thought, *would have a private room named after themselves in a place called Phineas MacDuff's House of Wonders?*

She tried the handle and found the door unlocked. Beyond it was an office, complete with a floor-to-ceiling bookcase of dusty volumes, another wall of smaller masks like the ones she had seen downstairs, two armchairs and an oversized desk set in front of a large window, behind which was a high-backed wooden chair with a jacket draped over it.

Zinnie crossed to the desk and quickly began to search. She found ledgers and letters, playbills and gilt-edged invitations, incomprehensible things that meant nothing to her. She worked her way down the four drawers on one side of the desk and then started on the other side. In the one at the top, she found a box of new, neatly rolled handkerchiefs and her heart gave a kick. Her hopes were dashed, however, when she realized the box was still sealed. If she opened it, surely MacDuff would realize that something was amiss.

Then the jacket over the back of the chair caught her eye – was there a kerchief already in it? She slipped her fingers into the top pocket and, sure enough, there one was – neatly folded. She shook it out to find it bore exactly what she'd hoped it would. In one corner was a name neatly embroidered in blue. Zinnie stuffed it into the bag with her other purloined objects and was about to close the drawer when she saw something pushed to the back of it that gave her pause.

It was a small, stained cardboard box, still half wrapped in the brown paper in which it had been delivered. The string that had tied it closed was loose. There was no address on the paper but there was a white tag attached to the string.

Something about the box made Zinnie pull it out and set it on the desk. The white tag bore a brief line of words, none of which she could read, and some numbers. She'd always found numbers easier than letters, and to her these looked like a date. Yesterday's date. She loosened the string enough to open the box a fraction and found herself staring at a pair of severed human ears.

For a moment she felt sick. Then she pulled herself together and looked in the drawer for a pencil and a sheet of paper.

CHAPTER 30

Zinnie quietly closed the door of MacDuff's office and went back the way she had come. By the time she reached Lady Sarah, Conan Doyle and the clerk again, they were in the final room on the ground floor. Lady Sarah seemed fascinated by a display of leather armour that had been worn by a small tribe of women in the Andaman Islands.

"I must get my seamstress to come here," she was murmuring, her nose almost pressed up against the cabinet glass. "That breastplate is precisely what I need for my next expedition. And those leg guards…"

Zinnie cleared her throat. "Lady Sarah," she said quietly. "You asked me to remind you of the time."

"Oh!" said the clerk, looking at Zinnie in surprise. "Forgive me – where did you come from?"

"My maid Zinthia you mean, young man?" said Lady

Sarah, straightening up. "Dear me, she arrived with us and has been behind me the entire time. Not very observant, are you?"

The clerk, red-faced, stuttered an apology, but Lady Sarah had already turned to Zinnie. "Should I be getting to my other appointment?"

"Yes, my lady, if you don't wish to be late."

"Very well, we must go. Thank you," she said to the clerk. "Conan Doyle here will reward you for your service. And I will be sure to tell all I meet that the House of Wonders will be well worth a visit."

"Th-thank you, my lady," stammered the clerk, following in the trio's wake as Lady Sarah swept ahead of them all towards the door. "But are you sure you won't stay until Mr MacDuff returns? He'll be sorry that he missed you."

"Quite sure, my good man," said Lady Sarah, as the clerk rushed ahead of them to open the door. "You did an admirable job, you know. I shall make sure MacDuff hears of it."

"You are too kind, my lady."

A moment later, they were back in Conan Doyle's carriage and rattling away from George Street.

"Well?" Conan Doyle asked, as soon as they were on the move. "That's a full bag you've got there, Miss Zinnie. What did you find?"

"You must let me out once we're round the corner," Zinnie said instead of answering. "There's somewhere I need to go straight away."

"But Zinnie, you can't rope us into nefarious deeds and not tell us their purpose!" Lady Sarah cried, throwing up her hands. "We must know – we must!"

"You will, I swear," Zinnie promised. "But not yet. After—"

"The seance?" Conan Doyle interrupted. "Is that what you were about to say?"

"The seance?" Lady Sarah asked. "What does the seance have to do with anything?"

Conan Doyle shook his head grimly. "Miss Zinnie intends to reveal all she knows tomorrow night, in front of what I think she is intending to be witnesses," he said.

"Not me," said Zinnie. "*I* won't need to reveal anything at all."

"Still, Miss Zinnie, you are in this – whatever it is – up to your neck," said Conan Doyle. "And that worries me greatly."

"Why?" Zinnie asked. "Because I'm a girl?"

"Not at all," he said darkly. "It's because I think you underestimate Phineas MacDuff."

"You've got that back to front, Mr Conan Doyle. He's the one who underestimates *me*."

"My dear girl – and with great respect – I doubt he even realizes you exist."

Zinnie flashed him a grin. "Exactly." She knocked on the carriage roof and raised her voice. "Stop, please. I need to get out."

"Zinnie," said Lady Sarah, as Zinnie jumped down to the pavement, the bag still over her shoulder. "I have great faith in you, whatever it is you're up to. But please, for me – be careful, won't you, my dear?"

"I will."

Lady Sarah nodded. "Then we shall see you tomorrow."

"Yes, my lady. I'll be waiting for you where Bank Street meets the Lawnmarket, at eleven o'clock sharp."

She began to run even before the horses had moved on, heading for the doctor's clinic. When she got there, Sadie was sitting beside Nell's bed, teaching the little girl her letters with the aid of a slate and a piece of chalk.

"Zinnie!" Nell cried, leaping out of bed so quickly that Sadie only just caught the slate before it crashed to the floor. "Why are you dressed as a maid?"

"Hello, pippin," Zinnie said, as the little girl flung her arms round her waist and hugged tightly. "Just fancied a change. What do you think?"

Nell considered, her head on one side and her eyes narrowed. "I think you look strange in a dress."

Zinnie laughed. "I think you're right. And as for you – well, aren't you looking just as fine and dandy as a daisy?"

Nell gave a smile as wide as the sky. "I feel right as rain," she declared. "And now I want to come home with you and Sadie. Can I come home, please? Please say I can, *please!*" She paused for breath and coughed a little as she caught it.

Zinnie hoisted the little girl up and into bed again.

"You're still coughing, pippin. Not quite right as rain yet, eh?"

"It's only because I was excited to see you!" Nell protested, indignant. "I'm not coughing much at all now, am I, Sadie? Tell her!"

Sadie looked up at Zinnie. "She is much better," she began and Nell made a happy noise. "*But* I don't think it'd be wise for you to come home just yet, Nell. A few more days here will do you the world of good."

Nell pouted and looked as if she might argue.

"Besides, if you come home now, it would spoil the surprise," Zinnie said quickly, aiming to avoid a tantrum. "You have to stay here with the doctor for at least another two nights, while Sadie and I put it all in place."

"A surprise!" Nell said, her eyes wide. "What is it?"

Zinnie laughed and ruffled Nell's already unruly hair. "If we told you, it wouldn't very well be a surprise, would it? You'll find out soon enough. But for now, I need you to stay here and I need Sadie to come with me to help me get it ready. All right?" She looked at Sadie and jerked her chin, indicating she wanted to talk to her sister out of Nell's hearing.

"What is it?" Sadie whispered, once they were standing outside the door. "What's going on?"

Zinnie handed her the scrap of paper on which she'd carefully written down the letters from the white tag. Her writing was shaky but she'd been as careful as she could be in her copying.

"What does that say?"

Sadie looked at the piece of paper and frowned. "Where did you get this? And why *are* you dressed as a maid again?"

"Just tell me what it says, Sadie."

"It says, 'The past is coming for you.'" Sadie looked up at her. "Zinnie. What *is* this?"

"It's nothing to worry about," Zinnie said, taking the piece of paper and putting it back in the pocket of her apron. "I'm going to need your help, though. Can you come with me?"

"What, now?"

Zinnie looked over Sadie's head to Nell, who was doodling with the chalk on the slate and humming to herself. "She's all right here, isn't she? Without you, I mean?"

"She'll be fine. Everyone here loves her. She's even managed to charm Mrs Collins."

Zinnie smiled. "That's good. Come on then."

CHAPTER 31

"What are we going to do about Nell?" Sadie asked, as they hurried back towards the castle.

"You heard her – she wants to come home," said Zinnie.

"But we don't *have* a home," Sadie pointed out. "Not really."

"Well, I'm not smart like you, Sadie. I can't read books or write letters. The doctor isn't going to offer to train *me* in medicine. I'll never go back to the orphanage, and I can't stand the idea of the poorhouse, so I'll make a home as best I can, where I can. For me and for Nell."

"The doctor said she was there when Lady Sarah offered to make you a maid in her house. Why can't you do that?"

They had reached the Mile. Zinnie stopped and turned to Sadie. "Nell's too young to be taken on as a maid. I can't leave her, can I? Anyway, there's still Aelfine to think of."

"You can't look after her properly, Zin!"

"She doesn't need me to! She can look after herself. She just needs to be with people who understand her, that's all. She just needs *help*. Nothing that's happened is her fault, it's MacDuff's!"

"I know, but—"

"What do you think would have happened to you if I'd listened to what everyone else thought?" Zinnie demanded. "If I'd listened to what they say about the Irish here, and even more what they say about a girl who knows every plant and how to use them? Or Nell? What if I'd listened to people who murmured about *Nell*?"

"I *know*," Sadie said, resting a hand on her arm. "And you'll never understand how much that means to me, Zinnie. But it's different with Aelfine. You must see—"

"It's not different! *She's* different, that's all, and that's what people don't like. They never do. She's not sick or stupid, Sadie. She doesn't need a doctor and she doesn't need to be locked up. She just needs patience and to be given a chance."

"But we can barely help ourselves. How are we going to help her?"

"We do our best," Zinnie said shortly. "Isn't that what I've always done for you? For Nell?"

Sadie's eyes filled with tears. "It is. I know it is."

Zinnie took a deep breath and pulled Sadie against her. "I'm so proud of you, do you know that?" she said into her sister's ear. "You're going to train with Doctor Jex-Blake and you're going to be a doctor, Sadie. A doctor! Imagine!"

"But what about you, Zinnie?"

Zinnie patted Sadie on the back. "Who knows? Maybe after all this is over I can set myself up as a professional finder-out of things. Not just for Conan Doyle but for whoever wants things found. Might earn enough to get a real room somewhere."

"With Aelfine and ... and Nell?"

Zinnie finally pulled away and looked down at Sadie with a frown. "Do you really want her to go into an orphanage? Would you really put her in one of those places?"

"No," Sadie said, wiping her eyes. "But Doctor Jex-Blake said ... she said there might be a way of arranging a private adoption. So she'd be in a proper house, with a proper family. We could still visit her, Zin, and she'd be safe and looked after."

Zinnie frowned. "A private adoption?"

Sadie nodded. "She said she'd arrange it herself. So that we'd know they'd be good people."

Zinnie looked away, up at the looming bulk of the castle. "Well," she said quietly, "I suppose that's something to think about."

Sadie looked relieved. "Then you will? You will think about it?"

"Of course I will. But it would be Nell that gets to decide anyway."

"She'll do anything you tell her to, Zin. You know that."

They reached the mouth of Writers' Court with Zinnie deep in thought. She'd been imagining the seance as a sort of line, beyond which everything would go back to normal. But she was beginning to realize that things would never be the same again. Their lives as they knew them were coming to an end and the sisters would never again be together in quite the same way.

She was so preoccupied by this thought that Sadie had to pull her out of the way to stop her walking straight into the man leaving Mary King's Close as they got to it. He was obviously in a hurry, charging up the broken stairs as if he were running from something. He was as out of place as Lady Sarah had been when she and the doctor had visited – more so, in fact, because he wore a top hat and cloak that flowed out behind him to become one with the shadows around him. He carried a heavy stick, topped with the silver head of a wolf. It was his face, though, that made Zinnie gasp. She turned away into the shadows, pulling Sadie with her as he strode past.

"What?" Sadie hissed. "What is it?"

"That was Phineas MacDuff!"

"What's he doing here?"

Zinnie wracked her brain. "Talbot must have told him about his visit yesterday. Why would he bring—" But she knew, before the thought had even had time to settle in her mind. "Oh no!"

She began to run, Sadie close behind her. They flew down the steps into the underground maze of Mary King's Close, struggling to hurry between the people crowded on the floor. Zinnie made straight for the street itself. It was still deserted but sounds were emanating from below – men's voices, bellowing. Bursting between each yell came a resounding screech.

"That's Ruby!" Zinnie hurtled down the steep alleyway, pulling out her little knife as she went. She reached the floorless room and could see, ahead, figures moving in the gloom: two men struggling. One of them had hold of Ruby and was trying to wrestle her into a cloth sack. The other was Talbot. He had Aelfine by one arm as she kicked and screamed, struggling to get to her pet. With his other hand, he was trying to help with the frantic monkey.

"Let them go!" Zinnie bellowed. "Let them go, right now!"

She dropped her bag and lunged at Talbot. She slashed at his arm and he roared as the blade cut deep enough to draw blood. He let go of Aelfine and she was flung backwards, stumbling towards the hole's edge.

"No!" Zinnie threw herself at Aelfine, grabbing at her as she plunged over the broken boards. She caught hold of the girl's arm but couldn't stop her falling. Over the edge of the void they both went, brick dust billowing around them as they plummeted into the dark. Zinnie heard Sadie scream her name. A second later, she crashed down beside

Aelfine, landing on what felt like a jagged pile of bricks and broken wood. She hit her head against something hard and saw stars sparking in the darkness. Her ears rang, and for a second she couldn't breathe, couldn't hear. Then sound rushed back in again – Sadie screaming, Ruby shrieking like a demon, Talbot and his man yelling.

Zinnie rolled towards Aelfine, patting for her in the dark. Her head hurt. So did her shoulder.

"Aelfine," she whispered, and tasted blood in her mouth.

Aelfine whimpered slightly. A shadow loomed far above them, at the edge of the hole. Zinnie covered Aelfine's mouth with her hand as Talbot searched the darkness for them. If they didn't move, if they didn't make a sound…

Ruby was still squawking, but it was muffled now – they'd managed to get her into the sack. Zinnie held her breath, tried to ignore the ache in her head.

"Let's go," Talbot said abruptly. "We've got one of them. We'll come back for the other with the rest of the men. If she's still alive. Or maybe she'll come looking for us instead, save us the trouble, eh?"

His shadow disappeared, but still Zinnie held her breath. The monkey's screeches faded along with Talbot's footsteps as he retreated with his prize.

There was a second of stillness. Then Sadie appeared at the lip of the void, her breath coming in harsh sobs.

"Zinnie!" she cried. "Where are you? Are you all right?"

Zinnie levered herself up, one hand against her sore head.

"I'm all right. Aelfine… Are you hurt?"

The girl sat up as Zinnie reached for her. "Ruby," she said tearfully. "They've got Ruby."

"I know – I'm sorry. But we'll get her back, I promise. Can you stand?"

They got up carefully, Aelfine still crying, although from what Zinnie could tell that was more about the loss of her pet than it was about being hurt.

It took them ages to find a way to climb out of the hole. Sadie helped to pull them out.

"You could both have been killed," she said, her voice still shaky as she hugged them.

"Yeah," Zinnie winced. "Let's not do that again if we can help it."

"Ruby," Aelfine moaned. "I've got to go after them. I've got to get her back!"

She went to follow the men, but Zinnie and Sadie both held her back.

"Stop," Zinnie said hoarsely, still winded. "Aelfine, you can't go after them. That's exactly what they want."

"But they'll hurt her! They'll—"

"They won't," Zinnie said. "She's too valuable to them for that. We'll get her back, I promise. I *promise*. But you have to stay here. You have to hide. You can't let them get you."

Aelfine collapsed in a heap and cried as if her world had ended.

CHAPTER 32

"That's it," said Sadie, wrapping her arms round Aelfine as the girl sobbed. "We have to cancel the seance. MacDuff knows it's Aelfine down here!"

"We can't cancel," Zinnie said. "If we don't do this now, he's going to get away with everything he's done and Aelfine will still be in danger."

"But Zinnie, how can we carry on?" Sadie demanded. "If he knows it's Aelfine, whatever we do, he's going to work out that the seance is some kind of trick. He'll have his own plan, won't he?"

"I know that," Zinnie said. "But I've got a plan too. And I need your help to make it work. I need both of you," she said, crouching beside Aelfine and putting her hands on the sobbing girl's shoulders. "We can beat him and we can get Ruby back, but only if we do this – together."

"I can't," Aelfine said, still crying. "I can't be the ghost without Ruby. I can't."

"You can," Zinnie promised. "I know you can and we'll be here to help you. This is the only way, Aelfine. If we don't do this, you're never going to be safe and we might never get Ruby back."

That made Aelfine sob even harder. Zinnie pulled her into a hug.

"Aelfine," Zinnie said softly. "What was your ma's name? I never asked you."

"Eliza," the girl wept, between gasps for breath. "Eliza Dumas."

"We can do this," she told both Aelfine and Sadie. "Together, we can do this. I know we can. We'll do it for your ma, Aelfine. We'll do it for Eliza. She deserves that, doesn't she?" Zinnie looked at Sadie over the distraught girl's head.

The sound of her mother's name seemed to have a calming effect on Aelfine. "Yes," she said. "We'll do it for Ma. And we'll get Ruby back. We will."

Sadie hesitated for another second and then nodded. "All right. What do you need me to do?"

Zinnie got to her feet. "First of all, Aelfine, I'm sorry – this is horrible – but I need you to tell me exactly where you saw MacDuff take your ma. Can you tell me where he left her body? Can you remember?"

Aelfine looked away. "Yes. I remember. She's under the

bridge at Dean, near the tree that has one –" she hiccupped a little but carried on – "one branch broken."

Zinnie hugged her tightly. "Thank you. I'll never ask you about that again. I promise. You're so brave, Aelfine. Are you ready for the next thing?"

Aelfine blinked, nodding.

"I need you to show Sadie how to get into that room on the other side of the hole without coming through this way. All right?"

Aelfine sniffed and gulped. "Yes," she said, looking at Sadie. "There's a lot of climbing."

"That's all right," Sadie said with a sigh. "I have a feeling that climbing is going to be the least difficult thing I'm going to have to do for this 'seance'."

"Brilliant," Zinnie said. "As for the rest of it … you're going to need these." She retrieved the bag she had brought from MacDuff's place and opened it, taking out the dress and scarf. The crystal ball and handkerchief she stuffed into her own pocket.

Aelfine gasped. "These are my ma's!"

Zinnie hugged her. "They are. I'm hoping the clothes will fit Sadie. She just needs to borrow them for tomorrow night."

Aelfine stared solemnly at the clothes, as if thinking hard. Then she looked up at Zinnie. "You want Sadie to pretend to be my ma. And you want me to show her how to be a ghost."

Zinnie smiled. "I said you were clever, didn't I?"

"Well, *Aelfine* might be," Sadie said. "But I'm as much in the dark as ever. What are you both talking about?"

Zinnie grinned. "I'll explain. Then you both need to get some rest. Tomorrow's going to be a long day and we're all going to have to be at our sharpest."

Later, once they had reached the hidden rooms beyond the broken floor and Zinnie had explained what needed to be done, she left the two girls alone and set off on her own errand.

As Zinnie made for Dean Village, part of her wished she'd asked Aelfine to come with her. But it would have been an awful ordeal to put the little girl through. Besides, Zinnie needed to know that it was possible for anyone to follow the directions Aelfine had given her.

The clouds had cleared and, as late as it was, there was still light in the sky. Soon it would be midsummer and once they were past it the days would begin closing in towards winter. Life in Mary King's Close was hard enough in good weather but, when the winds blew cold and brought the ice and snow at the tail end of the year, summer there felt like paradise.

Zinnie shivered at the thought of spending another winter in the close and wondered how many of her sisters would still be there with her. Part of her wished none of them would be, that Sadie, Nell and Aelfine would have found better places to be. She would miss her family terribly. But if they were safe and happy, she told herself, that would be fine.

Later still, Zinnie hurried back the way she had come in darkness, hearing the bell of St Giles clang out ten o'clock. She went into Writers' Court and ran up the stairs to Constance McQuirter's room, banging on the door only briefly before pushing her way in.

"No, no," Constance said, her voice dripping with sarcasm. "No need to wait for an answer, Zinnie. Just come straight in. My door is always open for you."

"Just wanted to check you were here, that's all," Zinnie said. "And that you haven't forgotten your engagement for tomorrow evening."

"'Engagement'," Constance repeated with a hoot of derisive laughter. "Talk about ideas above your station, Zinnie my girl. You almost make it sound respectable."

"Oh, I can make it sound a lot of things," Zinnie said. "But with you involved, 'respectable' could never be one of them."

"Watch it," the woman warned. "I'll be there. Then we're square and even, done and dusted. Right?"

"Might be," Zinnie agreed. "All depends how well you sell it."

The would-be medium threw up her hands in frustration. "Well, it'd be a damn sight easier if I knew what it was I was trying to sell and that's no mistake!"

"Trust me, you'll know," Zinnie said. "I've got to go. Things to do. Meet me at the top of the close at ten tomorrow and I'll take you down to where you need to be."

Zinnie turned for the door but Constance called her back.

"Wait," she said. "Zinnie – there's something going on, isn't there? Something more than just pulling the wool over the eyes of gullible rich folks."

Zinnie paused for a moment. "Aye," she said. "If you're not careful, McQuirter, you might end up doing a good deed. That'd be a first for you, wouldn't it?"

CHAPTER 33

At eleven o'clock the following night, Zinnie and Sadie stood side by side at the point where the steep ingress of Bank Street meets the Royal Mile. The rain was, for once, holding off, and the two girls were dry enough as they waited, ignoring the raucous calls of the hawkers packing up the last of their wares around them.

The first carriage to stop in front of them was Conan Doyle's. He jumped nimbly down to the pavement, slamming the door behind him as he waved the driver off.

"Ladies," he said, offering a brief bow. "And so here we are."

"Did you bring candles?" Zinnie asked. She had instructed him to tell all the attendees to bring at least one.

"Indeed I did," said Conan Doyle, producing two fresh candles from the pockets of his jacket.

A second carriage rattled to a halt beside them, far grander than Conan Doyle's. The footman jumped down to open the door and Lady Sarah appeared, wrapped in a voluminous teal-coloured cloak of satin that gleamed in the moonlight. She stepped out, and there behind her was Doctor Jex-Blake, dressed far more soberly in a plain grey dress beneath a black travelling cloak.

"Zinnie." Lady Sarah greeted her warmly. "And this is your sister Sadie, isn't it? We haven't been properly introduced, dear, but Sophia has been singing your praises. You're a promising potential student, so I hear."

Sadie bobbed an awkward half-curtsey but said nothing, obviously a little awed. Lady Sarah certainly did cut a striking figure amid the common bustle of the late-night Mile. Zinnie again tried to imagine her traipsing across sand or over mountains, and failed.

Another carriage pulled up and two gentlemen that Zinnie recognized from Lady Sarah's party alighted, both looking distinctly wary of their surroundings.

"Ah, Mr Danvers, Mr Arbuthnot, I am so glad you decided to join us," said Lady Sarah with great enthusiasm. "But not your good lady wives?"

"No," said Mr Danvers, looking a little awkward. "Begging your pardon, Lady Sarah, but myself and Arbuthnot here both judged this no suitable place for a lady."

"I take no offence, my dear man," said Lady Sarah

cheerfully. "No doubt, had he been alive, my husband would have held the same opinion. One of the advantages of having been left alone in life is the luxury to do just as I please."

A final carriage appeared. The hard knot in Zinnie's stomach tightened even further, for it could only belong to one person. A moment later and MacDuff himself stood with the rest of the party, his dark eyebrows drawn together in a forbidding frown.

"Well, Conan Doyle," he said in that broad American accent that Zinnie was sure was not even close to being his own. "You were keen for me to attend this – whatever it turns out to be – and here I am. I pray it will be nothing worse than a waste of time."

Zinnie's skin crawled as she looked at the man who had killed at least one person and been so eager to reduce Aelfine to nothing more than an animal in a cage. Part of her wanted to plunge her knife into his belly, but more than anything she wanted justice for Aelfine and Eliza. She had to get this evening right for it all to work the way she had planned.

"Are we sure about this?" Arbuthnot spoke up. He looked Zinnie and Sadie up and down. "I for one am not at all convinced that putting ourselves at the mercy of the sort of ... *person* we shall find in these parts is a good idea."

"Oh, but there will be surely none of us who wish to turn back *now*," said Lady Sarah, looking round the little semicircle. "We are all here and ready to go, after all. Who would want to waste the journey?"

Zinnie noticed a look pass between the gentlemen which suggested that they would have happily done just that, but neither of them wished to appear less courageous than the women in their midst.

"Excellent," said Lady Sarah, after the moment had passed in silence. "I'm sure you menfolk can protect Sophia and I should the need arise, eh? So, let us be away."

"I'm not coming with you," said Sadie. "I've got to get back to the clinic, to Nell."

"Oh," said Doctor Jex-Blake. "I'm sure that's not necessary, Sadie. Mrs Collins will see to your sister."

"I know, but I want to be with her," Sadie said. "And to be honest –" she bit her lip – "it scares me, so it does. The ghost…"

Zinnie gave her a hug. "Not to worry. Go – be with Nell. Give her a kiss from me and tell her I'll see her soon."

"Oh, do let's get on with it!" MacDuff huffed. "Do we really need these ragged excuses for children as guides? Surely we can find our own way. Let them *both* go."

"I wouldn't advise that, MacDuff," said Conan Doyle, before Zinnie could turn on him. "I'll wager these girls know this place better than you know your own moustache."

Sadie let Zinnie go and disappeared into the bustle of the street. Zinnie turned, gave MacDuff the sweetest smile she could muster and led the peculiar assembly down the Mile.

"Light your candles now, please," she said, as she stood on the top step of the entrance into the underground closes. "And stay together. Below lurks danger, but also Madame Khartoubian and the absolute truth."

She thought she heard a small snort of derision coming from MacDuff's direction, but ignored it and began to descend the steps.

Zinnie and Sadie had spent most of the day attempting to make the path down to the deepest recesses of the close as clear as possible. There was nothing they could do, however, about the destitute inmates of the place, or the filth that was ingrained in the walls and – where they were still intact – the floors.

Zinnie, looking back from the head of the column as they moved out on to the close itself, saw Mr Danvers holding a kerchief over his nose and mouth to counteract the choking smell. Zinnie couldn't blame him and, as she saw MacDuff search for his own handkerchief, she thought again of little Nell, looking so radiant with health in her clean hospital bed. *I can't bring her back here*, she thought to herself, yet again. *I just can't*. She saw MacDuff frown a little as he realized his handkerchief was missing.

"Mind your step, if you please," she called back up the hill. "The path is steep and uneven. Don't want you all going teeth-over-toes."

When they reached the ruined room in which the seance would be held, Zinnie stood aside.

"Please, place your candles with the others," she said, ushering her 'guests' inside, "and stay on the path until you reach the table. The floor is dangerous anywhere else."

The 'path' had been Sadie's idea – a line of fallen house bricks and chunks of half-rotten timber laid in two parallel lines around the near edge of the great hole in the floor. Between them had been created a narrow space to walk, lined with as many lit candle stubs as the girls had been able to collect. The dim light these gave off flickered yellow and was just enough to lead their guests towards where Constance McQuirter, now fully transformed into Madame Khartoubian, sat at a round 'table' that the girls had cobbled together from scavenged planks. From the ruined doorway, it seemed as if the medium were sitting on the last tiny outcrop of solid ground hanging over the edge of a bottomless abyss surrounded by darkness.

"My goodness," murmured Lady Sarah, pausing at the start of the path and gazing upon the setting for this most unusual of evenings.

Zinnie had to admit that even knowing what she did the effect was striking. If ever a spirit were to inhabit a place on earth, this would surely be it.

"Please," called Madame Khartoubian in her soft French accent, strange shadows cast by the candlelight dancing across her face. "Be not afraid. Approach, my friends, for the spirits of this place are waiting for us. I feel them pressing in, trying to find a conduit into our realm."

One by one, the party added their candles to the stones and made their way down the path, into the darkness.

CHAPTER 34

With everyone seated, there was just one space left at the table. This Zinnie took herself.

"At last," said Madame Khartoubian, "we are all assembled. The spirits are restless: the witching hour will soon be upon us. Let us begin."

The Ouija board came first. Madame Khartoubian asked questions, trying to call out to the ghost that had been haunting the close. But instead of answers there was silence. The medium was not to be bested, however – she filled the pauses with messages for those at the table, answers to questions that had not been asked, purportedly from 'beyond the veil'.

"Please, ladies and gentlemen, the spirits are waiting," she crooned at one point. "What questions would you have them answer?"

Clearly, Zinnie thought, Constance had run out of ideas of her own. More than once, she glanced at Zinnie, as if to ask what she was waiting for. Zinnie could not have told her, even if she'd been so inclined. Aelfine and Sadie were working to their own cue, and not even Zinnie knew what that was. She'd told them it would work better that way.

"If I look as surprised as the rest, so much the better," she'd said.

Still, it must be getting towards midnight now, she thought, anxiety twisting in her gut. *What if something's gone wrong? What if Aelfine is refusing to do it without Ruby or—*

Then a gasp went up from Lady Sarah.

"It rises!" she cried. "The spirit is there, see!"

The heads of all those at the table turned. The 'spirit' shimmered in the darkness, floating in mid-air. The black hood was dipped low over its darkened face, only its flickering lips visible. Gasps rippled round the table.

"Holy Mother," cursed Constance, momentarily losing control of Madame Khartoubian's careful French accent. "It truly is a spirit of the dead!"

Zinnie shot a quick glance at MacDuff, who was sitting with his lips in a firm line, his eyes narrowed.

He's been waiting for this, Zinnie realized, her stomach twisting.

"Talk to us, spirit," Constance cried, sliding into her rehearsed lines. "Tell us what troubles you!"

"I am the ghost of Mary King's Close," came the answer

in Aelfine's rough voice, echoing across the void as if coming from all places at once. "Great injustice calls me forth. I am unsettled and wander, restless—"

A commotion behind them interrupted Aelfine's speech. Zinnie turned towards the end of the lit path. A figure had appeared, a sack wriggling in its arms. It was Talbot!

"Finally," said MacDuff loudly, from across the table. "Let this ridiculous farce be ended!"

Talbot laughed, an ugly sound. He opened the sack a fraction and something within screeched and shrieked, a horrible demonic sound that grated against the nerves. Ruby struggled and squalled, but Talbot held her fast, shaking the poor little monkey with vicious glee.

Oh no, Zinnie thought. *No!*

"*Ruby!*"

Aelfine's scream cut across the void, as if a firecracker had been lit in the darkness. The 'spirit' vanished and there came the sound of scrabbling.

"Ruby!" Aelfine cried again, and the monkey screeched back even as the sound of swiftly clambering footsteps grew nearer. "I'm coming!"

"No!" Zinnie shouted, lurching to her feet as she realized what was about to happen. "Aelfine! No, don't! Stay away!"

But it was too late. MacDuff was already out of his seat and ahead of Zinnie. Aelfine appeared from the darkness, thinking of nothing but her poor captured pet. MacDuff reached out and grabbed her by the back of the neck.

"Here!" he cried. "Here is your so-called 'spirit'!" MacDuff thrust Aelfine towards one of the candles so that her face was illuminated for the other guests to see.

"What?" gasped Lady Sarah. "What is this?"

"This is the idiot wretch who stole my monkey!" MacDuff bellowed, shaking Aelfine as if she were an errant dog. "Look at her, the ungrateful whelp!"

"Let her go!" Zinnie yelled.

"I will not!" MacDuff shouted, backing away towards the edge of the hole as Zinnie approached. "That she should steal from *me*, who clothed and fed her! Who gave her a home away from the circus instead of sending her to an asylum, where she rightfully belongs!"

"Mr MacDuff, please!" This time the voice came from Doctor Jex-Blake. "Whatever she has done, she is also just a child!"

"She's done nothing!" Zinnie cried, as Aelfine sobbed and Ruby continued to screech. "Nothing except escape a prison he made for her. Nothing but run from a—"

"And these disgusting, ragged reprobates," MacDuff bellowed again, drowning out Zinnie's voice, "these vagrant excuses for children who helped her! I will have them all jailed for their crimes!"

"Let me go!" Aelfine screamed, struggling. "He killed my mother! He wants to kill me too! Help me! Help—"

"See what absurdities the idiot spouts!" MacDuff shouted. "More proof that she should be locked away with a gag about her mouth for the rest of her days!"

Zinnie rushed at MacDuff with her knife drawn, but Conan Doyle saw what she meant to do and grabbed her before she could reach him, trying to pull her back.

"She's telling the truth!" Zinnie shouted. "MacDuff is a murderer! He killed Aelfine's mother and—"

MacDuff silenced her by striking Zinnie across the mouth with the back of his closed fist. Pain exploded along her jaw as her head jerked back and she tasted blood in her mouth.

"MacDuff!" Conan Doyle protested. "How dare you—"

Another scream, far louder than the rest, split the pandemonium. It was Constance McQuirter.

"Another ghost!" she shrieked, in real terror. "A true spectre! See!"

Zinnie lifted her head, blinking, as MacDuff swung round to look. There, floating above the non-existent floor, was the pale, flickering figure of a woman. She wore a striped dress and her hair was hidden beneath a red scarf, her face indistinct in the shadows.

"Ma!" Aelfine screamed, and then fainted clean away.

CHAPTER 35

"It's another trick!" cried MacDuff.

"Miss Zinnie –" Conan Doyle gripped both of her shoulders – "is this more play-acting?"

"No, I swear," she told him, staring at the ghost as she sank to her knees.

"She's lying!" MacDuff spat.

Conan Doyle didn't believe it. "Look at her, man! She's terrified. Whatever this is, I don't think—"

"Hush," Lady Sarah cried, pointing towards the ghost. "It wishes to speak!"

The ghost opened its mouth, weaving its head from side to side as if it were searching the darkness for something familiar. "My daughter," it moaned in a voice that drew out each syllable as if it were a song. "My poor, dear daughter, where are you? Aelfine! Aelfine!"

At the sound of her name, Aelfine stirred and came to herself. Weakly, she looked up into the darkness and cried out again. "Ma! That's my own dear ma!"

"It's a lie!" MacDuff snapped, shaking Aelfine again, but the others of the party shushed him into silence. Doctor Jex-Blake stepped forward and forced MacDuff to loosen his hands from round the girl, gently helping her to her feet.

"What makes you think it is your mother, child?" she asked. "How do you recognize her? Her face is not clear."

"It's her dress," Aelfine sobbed. "The dress she always wore when telling fortunes. And she wrapped her head so, always."

"Rubbish," spluttered MacDuff, and Zinnie could hear the change in his accent. His words no longer held the broad twang of American. "The idiot is lying, I tell you! Surely you'll not believe the words of this degenerate girl over mine?"

"I believe there is no harm in listening, MacDuff," Conan Doyle said. "After all, something has brought this restless spirit from the hereafter. By the way, you seem to have become Australian all of a sudden."

MacDuff opened his mouth, blinking in shock, and then collected himself. "I will stay here no longer and listen to this!"

The ghost gave a pitiful moan, raising her hands to her neck and then pointing at MacDuff. "Murderer!" the apparition cried. "My murderer is at hand!"

MacDuff spun on his heels to leave, but Danvers and Arbuthnot stopped him.

"Get out of my way!"

"We cannot simply ignore an allegation of murder, MacDuff," one of them said. "Even if it comes from beyond the grave."

"This is absurd!" MacDuff spluttered. "You're all being taken in by a trick, nothing more!"

"Murderer!" cried the ghost again. "He wrapped his hands about my neck when I said I would leave. He squeezed the life from my body without a single thought of remorse in his ungodly mind, because I knew the truth of his past and he wanted my daughter for his terrible house!"

"Where are you?" Aelfine begged, reaching out her arms as if her mother could pick her up. "Where is your body?"

"Lying in unconsecrated ground," the ghost moaned. "Unmarked, discarded like so much waste."

"But where?" asked Lady Sarah. "Where would we find your body, were we to look for it?"

"I lie beneath the bridge they call Dean," said the ghost. "Beside the Water of Leith there is an oak tree with branches broken on its eastern side. Between it and a fallen slab of sandstone you will find me in a shallow grave."

Zinnie looked at MacDuff, who was staring at the apparition with a new kind of horror. "It's not possible," he whispered.

"What is not possible, MacDuff?" asked Conan Doyle.

MacDuff came to his senses and shook his head, puffing out his chest. "It's not possible that sensible citizens such as yourselves have been taken in by such trickery. I even unmasked the culprits, yet still you are gullible enough to believe these inbred fools."

"Well, I believe there is but one way to be sure of the truth," said Conan Doyle. "And that is for us to journey to the Dean Bridge this instant and see whether the spirit is speaking the truth."

"What?" MacDuff said, flabbergasted. "You would have me, an upstanding citizen, dragged through the night to traipse about a riverbank on the whim of an illusion?"

"How do you know it's an illusion?" asked Doctor Jex-Blake.

"I will prove it to you!" MacDuff snarled, and with that he snatched up one of the candles and tried to pick his way over the broken floor. The void prevented him, however, and though he tried to find a way across, he could not. Still the ghost of Aelfine's mother lingered, flickering and floating in the midnight dark.

Eventually, MacDuff came back, defeated yet still defiant. "It is no matter," he said. "I have had enough of this ridiculous charade. I am leaving and I'm taking my property with me. Stop me and there'll be hell to pay."

He moved towards the door again, grabbing at Aelfine to drag her with him.

"You can't take her," said Doctor Jex-Blake. "No person

is property and that child especially is not."

"Oh, do shut up, woman," MacDuff growled, his accent slipping again in the heat of the moment. "Go and play at some new profession. There is no court in the land that will say I've not been wronged."

"Maybe not in this land yet," said a new voice from the doorway. "But in another you are most definitely the villain, Phineas MacDuff. Or should I say … James Fowler?"

A sudden hush fell over the assembled company. Zinnie turned. The newcomer was tall and wore a wide-brimmed hat tipped to one side, a gold earring in his single ear.

"Hobart!" hissed MacDuff.

Zinnie stared in shock. She recognized that name! The young lawman who had tried to stop the Queensland Kings from robbing the train – and had paid the price for standing up to them by losing his ear.

The man tore his hat from his head and a gasp rippled round the room at the sight of the ugly scar where his right ear should be. "Twelve years I've spent tracking you, Fowler. When your old muckers got out of jail, I knew they'd want to find you too. I followed them – could have had them locked up again at any time, but I let them find you for me instead. No way I was going to let the Queensland Kings escape justice a second time. Even if I had to deliver that justice with my own hands."

"It was you…" MacDuff whispered. "*You* sent the ears."

The man grinned, though it soon faded into an

expression of such coldness that even Zinnie shivered. "Nice touch, eh? What did you think, that they'd come from beyond the grave?"

"You've no proof," MacDuff declared. "You're just another homeless drunk wandering the streets. Who would believe your word beside mine?"

"I might," spoke up Lady Sarah, her strong voice echoing in the cavernous dark. "After all, there's a body, isn't there? And we know where it is. The spirit has told us."

"The spirit!" MacDuff scoffed. "There's no spirit, only children playing games."

"But we have both of them here," Lady Sarah pointed out. "So, if that ghost *is* a trick, who is playing it?"

"Look," said Madame Khartoubian. "The spectre – it's gone."

Zinnie looked up. Sure enough, the flickering spirit had vanished. All was silent apart from the guttering of the candle stubs, gasping their last in the damp air of the ruined room.

"She delivered her message," said the medium in a hushed tone. "She will have no need to return unless you choose not to heed it."

"Trick or not," said Hobart, "MacDuff has escaped a lifetime of crimes and must not go free again."

"From what I understand, Hobart," Conan Doyle said gravely, "you have just confessed to murder yourself. Four times over, man."

Hobart dipped his chin. "Aye, sir, you are right. I was a good lawman once. But the Queensland Kings changed that when they attacked that train. I'd do it all over again to see them served right. I'd do it for my Elsie, who had her life ripped away by thugs not fit to clean her boots."

"Elsie?" Zinnie said. "Isn't that your wife's name? She was with you on the train, wasn't she? I remember that from the news report Mr Conan Doyle read to me."

A shadow passed across Hobart's frowning face. "She was. We'd only been married two days. That was our honeymoon trip. My wages didn't amount to much, but the tramway company said they'd gift me the trip into the mountains where a friend of ours had a little cabin if I kept an eye on what they were carrying during the journey." He looked away. "She never recovered from her injuries. Died a week later."

There was silence as those gathered took in the tragedy of Hobart's words.

"I'm sorry," Zinnie said. "That's a terrible thing."

"It was. And it made me a terrible person in turn. But now, once Fowler is behind bars, I'm done. I'll sign my name to a full confession. I just want him –" at this Hobart jabbed a finger in MacDuff's direction – "to pay. No court will convict him over crimes for which I have no proof from so long ago. But if there's a body that can prove he's guilty anew, we must find it."

"We will," said Conan Doyle, his voice solemn.

"Come, all. Let us see what we shall find beneath the arches of Dean Bridge."

There was a screech and then the sound of running feet. Talbot had dropped Ruby and made a run for it.

CHAPTER 36

Aelfine didn't want to go to Dean Bridge with everyone else. She and Ruby retreated into the darkness, taking with them Zinnie's promise to return soon. Zinnie knew that Sadie would be waiting for them in the hidden room beyond the void.

"Zinnie," said Doctor Jex-Blake, as Lady Sarah's carriage followed Conan Doyle's along Queensferry Street. "Did you know what was going to happen?"

Zinnie turned to her with a frown. "How could I have known?"

"The first ghost. You knew that one wasn't real, at least."

Zinnie studied her hands. "Yes," she confessed. "We did it to expose MacDuff. Because we needed to find a way to save Aelfine before he found her."

"But why all the subterfuge?" Lady Sarah asked.

"Why not just tell the police?"

Zinnie looked up. "With my face all over those wanted posters? How could I? And as if they'd believe the likes of us anyway."

Lady Sarah frowned. "Then … the second ghost…"

Zinnie shared a look with Constance. "We'd never had a real medium there before," she said softly. "Aelfine's poor ma must have been out there, wanting to get through, but she couldn't until Madame Khartoubian here gave her a … what's it called?"

Constance's eyes narrowed very slightly. "A conduit. From the spirit world to this one."

Zinnie nodded. "That's right. One of them."

"My goodness," muttered Lady Sarah, and for a moment Zinnie felt a pang of guilt at her deceit, but she shook it off. It was worth a little dishonesty, she told herself, to catch MacDuff. She was so proud of Sadie. Her performance had been just as good as Aelfine's.

As if she'd heard her thoughts, the doctor spoke again. "Zinnie. Your friend Aelfine…"

"She's our sister," Zinnie said, turning to look out of the window at the darkened houses as they passed. It was touching 1 a.m. Witching hour was almost over.

There was a moment of silence. Zinnie felt a great chasm open up in her heart, because even if they had beaten MacDuff she had failed Aelfine. Everyone knew about her and everyone had seen her, and Zinnie did not know how she would now keep her safe.

"She's not an idiot," Zinnie said, in answer to a question she had not been asked. "She's clever at a lot of things. She sees everything and she's quick. She's just a little different, that's all."

"I think there is a word for what Aelfine has," said the doctor quietly. "I recently read a paper by a John Langdon Down, in which he describes a set of characteristics that a certain type of person has. He calls it 'Down's syndrome'. The sketches that he included of his subjects lead me to think that maybe that's what Aelfine has."

"What does it matter what it's called?" Zinnie asked, as the carriage neared Dean Village. "She's Aelfine and she's my sister. No one should need to call her anything beyond that."

"I think I agree with you, Zinnie," said Doctor Jex-Blake. "But I also think that Aelfine needs help. That's something *you* can agree with, isn't it?"

The carriages were slowing, rattling to a halt. Zinnie waited for theirs to stop before she looked at the doctor again. "It depends what you mean by help," she said. "The sort where she's fed and watered but put in a cage to perform for the rest of her life? Or the sort where she's fed and watered and put in a room with a locked door and nothing to do?"

She opened the carriage door and jumped to the ground before Doctor Jex-Blake could reply. The men were already at the edge of the bridge, holding up oil lamps taken from the carriages. Below, the Water of Leith was crashing heavily along its route, swollen by the recent rain.

"The ladies should stay here," Conan Doyle was saying. "The ground is too steep and treacherous for them to go any further."

"Curses," said Lady Sarah. "I should have worn my Hawaiian riding habit."

"Hobart," said Conan Doyle. "Keep hold of MacDuff."

"Oh aye," said the one-eared man. "I'll not let him get away this time, believe me."

MacDuff – or Fowler, as he truly was – looked defiant. "This is ridiculous," he spluttered. "This place is known for suicides. Even if you find a body, the law will know that's all it is. You have no *proof*."

Zinnie ignored him. "I'm not staying behind," she told Conan Doyle. "I'm coming too."

The land beside the bridge dropped steeply away from the sandstone arches, and even with the lights it was hard for any of them to see where to set foot. The undergrowth grabbed at them, tangled round their legs and arms, conspired to drop branches before their feet.

"We should have waited until morning," muttered Arbuthnot.

"And let an innocent victim lie out here another night?" said Conan Doyle. "She's been left too long already. For shame, man."

Down and down the column went, Zinnie bringing up the rear. She wondered how they would find any landmarks at all in the darkness, let alone a single broken tree and a dropped stone amid the mess around them. The sound of the river grew louder, tripping over itself, splashing and crashing through the mired darkness. Zinnie looked behind her, back up the slope to the road, and saw the silhouetted figures of Lady Sarah, Doctor Jex-Blake and Constance McQuirter standing by the roadside next to Hobart and MacDuff.

In the gloom ahead, a shout went up, a cry of, "The tree is here, an oak with branches down to the east!", and then the search was on properly, until Danvers found the stone by falling over it and landing in the mud.

There was a moment of commotion as he was helped to his feet and then a sliver of silence as the light from the lamps merged together to give a great, yellow glow.

It was Conan Doyle who said quietly, "Here she is."

A scattering of leaves and twigs had blown across the body, which was almost entirely hidden from sight by the trees and bushes around it. Zinnie stared at the sorry bundle. The woman's dress was striped, like the one worn by the ghost who had led them to this unhallowed place. Her dark hair was covered by a scarf.

"You should turn aside, Miss Zinnie," Conan Doyle said gently. "This is no sight for a young lady."

She looked up at him, her eyes clear, and said, "I am not afraid and I'm no lady. I want to see."

The men lifted the body gently and, between them, they carried her back up the slope to the road where the ladies were waiting.

"Heaven preserve us," whispered Lady Sarah, clapping one hand over her mouth as they reappeared. "It was all true."

The men laid the body on the road and held their lamps over it as Conan Doyle knelt at the woman's head. Her white face was smeared with mud. Arthur took the kerchief from his top pocket and wiped away the worst of the dirt from her eyes, lips and cheeks. The visage that emerged was lined around the eyes, gentle.

"We should have brought the girl, her daughter," said one of the other gentlemen. "She could have acted as witness."

"And submit the poor child to seeing her mother thus?" Doctor Jex-Blake said. "That would have been a terrible cruelty."

"It's a suicide," MacDuff scoffed. "Even if it is the woman you say it is. She'll have run away and thrown herself off the bridge because she couldn't bear the truth of her progeny. Any judge will agree and you will find no proof to say otherwise."

Zinnie was watching Conan Doyle. He had continued to wipe away debris, moving from the dead woman's face to her neck. Even in the greasy light of the oil lamps, it was possible to see that her neck was tilted at an unnatural angle and, moreover, that there were marks on her pale skin.

"Doctor Jex-Blake," he called softly. "Please, a second opinion. What do these look like to you?"

The doctor's skirts rustled as she moved closer to the corpse, crouching to get a better look. "I'd say they look like fingermarks," she said.

"As from someone gripping the victim's neck in the act of strangulation?"

"Yes," said the doctor. "I would say exactly that."

"This is still none of it any proof!" MacDuff insisted. "They could be anyone's fingermarks – her idiot daughter's even! Perhaps she flew into a rage, as those with a mental imbalance are apt to do, and slew her mother herself! You cannot blame this on me!"

"There's something in her hand," Zinnie said.

Conan Doyle examined both of Eliza Dumas's hands and found one clenched tightly closed. He prised open the fingers and pulled out what had been clutched inside them. It was a square of white fabric, wrapped round something and dirtied by its sojourn amid the mud of the Water of Leith. He opened it out to reveal a small crystal sphere.

Constance McQuirter gasped. "The fortune-teller's crystal ball! It must be her!"

"And this rag is a handkerchief," said Conan Doyle. "There is embroidery here, a name… Wait, I think I can read what it says…"

Phineas MacDuff gasped. His hand went to his top pocket, looking for something that wasn't there. Then he looked straight at Zinnie, who glared back at him with a steady and unwavering gaze.

"Thief," he whispered hoarsely.

"Murderer," she hissed back.

He tried to escape, wrenching himself out of Hobart's grasp and lurching in the direction of the church at the west end of Dean Bridge, but Zinnie stopped him before he could get far. She launched herself at his legs, wrapping her arms round his knees and bringing him down in a struggling heap against the loose shingle of the road, her knees crashing painfully into the ground. Hobart and Danvers dragged him to his feet as Conan Doyle smoothed flat the kerchief and read the name embroidered at its corner.

Phineas MacDuff.

CHAPTER 37

7th July 1879

THE SCOTSMAN

MURDERER BROUGHT TO JUSTICE

REVELATIONS FROM BEYOND THE GRAVE LEAD
TO DRAMATIC SCENES AT DEAN BRIDGE

Dean Village, Edinburgh. The respectable classes of the city are today rocked by the revelation that an unrepentant thief and murderer has attempted to infiltrate their midst. Phineas MacDuff, owner of new George Street attraction MacDuff's House of Wonders, which had been set to open imminently amid great anticipation, has been unmasked as a thief, a fugitive and a cold-blooded murderer.

Amid scenes of confusion at a seance organized by Lady Sarah Montague and held in the derelict recesses of Mary King's Close, MacDuff was unmasked as being, in truth, James Fowler, former member of a notorious gang of thieves calling themselves the Queensland Kings. In 1867, the gang derailed a train below the Little Liverpool mountain range in Queensland. They then attacked and made off with £20,000. Four of the five assailants were later caught and jailed, but the fifth – Fowler, later to rename himself MacDuff – escaped, taking the money with him.

For the next twelve years, the newly renamed Phineas MacDuff roamed the globe, using his ill-gotten gains to build up the collection that would eventually become the House of Wonders. However, he did not bank on the fact that his former gang-mates, thirsty for revenge, would break out of jail and come looking for him. Neither did he spare a thought for the determination of Mr Carlson Hobart, a police constable aboard the train robbed by the Queensland Kings, who had perhaps even more of a reason to track Fowler down – his young wife had been fatally injured during the train derailment and he himself had suffered the brutal removal of his left ear.

Hobart's quest took on its own form of justice. He murdered the first four of the Queensland Kings, sending their ears to his final intended victim – James Fowler himself. In the meantime, however, Fowler's criminal nature had reasserted himself and he had killed again.

A woman called Eliza Dumas, a fortune-teller by trade, had refused to allow her daughter to perform in the House of Wonders. Fowler killed her in a fit of rage, but had not banked on the persistence of the dead. It was the ghost of Dumas herself, raised by the skilled medium Madame Khartoubian, who damned Fowler by pointing the way to her own body.

Fowler and Hobart are now in custody and awaiting their turn before the magistrates. Whereas it may in some respects be possible to experience pity for Hobart, however, there is surely none to spare for James Fowler.

The news was too late for the morning papers, but the evening ones were full of the apprehension of the robber and murderer Phineas MacDuff – or, as he should be rightly known, James Fowler. Zinnie couldn't read the words but she stared at the sketch that the *Scotsman*'s artist had put together for the front page. It showed Dean Bridge, the water rushing beneath it, the crescent moon shining above it and their little band of searchers making their way through the undergrowth, looking for Eliza Dumas' body. It was the talk of the town that the House of Wonders had, in fact, been the very opposite of wonderful, and that its owner was himself a particular kind of curiosity – the sort that polite society thrill to talk about, but would rather not admit had ever been part of their own circle.

It was in the foyer of one such circle that Zinnie observed the artist's work, because Lady Sarah had sent a messenger with a note to say she wanted to talk to her. Zinnie did not really want to see Lady Sarah. She had a feeling there were many awkward questions to come and she would prefer not to have to face any of them. But still she had answered the gentle summons, and now found herself waiting in that huge, gilded foyer.

"My dear Zinnie," came the lady's voice from above. Zinnie looked up to see her descending the great stairs, looking as striking as ever in a dress as scarlet as the wings of her macaw. "I am so glad you're here: if you had not visited me, I would have come looking for you. Let's go into the sitting room. The fire is lit in there so it'll be warmer. We have much to discuss."

To Zinnie's surprise, it wasn't the events of the previous night that Lady Sarah wanted to talk about, but the future of Zinnie and her sisters.

"Now that hideous man has been caught," said Lady Sarah, settling herself by the fire, "we must get to the bottom of why you are so resistant to my help."

Zinnie shifted uncomfortably. "It's not that I'm not grateful, my lady," she said. "But—"

"It is Aelfine that worries you the most, isn't it?" Lady Sarah interrupted. "That poor little girl who had no one to defend her once her own mother had been murdered."

"She has me," Zinnie said. "She has Sadie, and she'll have Nell too, when they meet."

Lady Sarah smiled and took a sip of tea as she looked at Zinnie over the fine china rim of the cup.

"You say that she is quite clever, in some ways."

"Yes," said Zinnie. "In most ways. She's just ... *different*, that's all."

"She is not violent or prone to rages?"

"No. She's gentle. You've seen how she is with Ruby."

"Ah yes," said Lady Sarah with a laugh. "The monkey."

"That's another reason she could never go to an asylum," Zinnie said. "I think they would both die if they were separated for any length of time. They love each other like ... well, like sisters."

Lady Sarah nodded and put down her cup and saucer. "There is also the matter of Nell, your youngest sister," she said. "I know from Doctor Jex-Blake that you have a horror of the orphanages and that she has suggested a private adoption instead."

Zinnie's gut twisted at the thought of little Nell being put with strangers. But what could she do? Taking Nell back to Mary King's Close would only leave her open to getting sick again. Besides, Talbot was still out there and, however hard she tried, Zinnie wouldn't be able to keep all of them safe from him all the time. And yet...

"You don't like that idea, either, though, do you?" Lady Sarah asked, watching her carefully.

"I won't be with her," Zinnie blurted. "I won't be there to make sure they treat her well. She's my sister but I wouldn't be able to – to keep her safe!"

Lady Sarah nodded. She stared at the fire for a moment. "What if *I* were to be the one to adopt her?"

For a moment Zinnie thought she must have misheard. "Y-you?"

"And Aelfine too. Sadie and yourself as well, for that matter. Would you trust me to look after you all? Would you like to live in Montague House, with me?"

Zinnie's mind was spinning so fast that she was having trouble keeping up with what Lady Sarah was saying.

Surely she couldn't mean it? To have them all living here? How could that possibly ever—

"I do mean it," Lady Sarah said, as if she could read Zinnie's mind. "Look at this place, Zinnie. It is too big for just me, especially when I'm away for such long periods of time. If the four of you come here – five, sorry, of course I must count Ruby too – then you will all be safe, always. Aelfine can be looked after as much or as little as she needs, and will always have a home. Nell can enter school when she's old enough. Sadie can train with Sophia. And you…"

She stopped and Zinnie looked up. "What about me?"

"Well, I once asked if you wanted to be a maid here, Zinnie, but now I realize that it is not an occupation that would suit you."

Zinnie blinked, surprised by the stab of disappointment in her gut. Lady Sarah didn't want her, after all? "Oh."

"Having seen you in action – how resourceful you are, how resilient and brave – I have come to think that instead you would be a perfect travelling companion."

Zinnie forgot to breathe. "A – what?"

Lady Sarah leaned forward with a grin that lit up her face. "What do you say, Zinnie? Will you come with me to South America?"

There was a moment of silence before Zinnie managed to speak. "But why?" she asked in a whisper. "Why would you do all that, for us?"

Lady Sarah smiled. "Because I can and because I should.

And –" she looked down at her elegant hands folded in her lap – "because I hope it means that I will not grow old wondering what I could have done differently to leave something good behind me. One thinks about that more and more, you know, as one ages."

Zinnie looked into the crackling fire, still stunned.

"I am so very grateful that Arthur introduced us, Zinnie," Lady Sarah said softly. "I think it will do all of us a very great service to have each other in our lives. He's very taken with the idea of an intrepid group of children who know the streets of a city in a way no one else can. His imagination is as sharp as his intellect, you know. Don't be surprised if you turn up in one of his stories one day. Anyway. You will talk to your sisters about my proposal?" Lady Sarah asked. "And you will think about your own future? South America will not be easy, I grant you, but I have a fancy you are more than up to the challenge."

Zinnie carried on staring into the fire. There was a lot to take in, but really how could any of them turn down such an offer? "Of course I will," she said.

Lady Sarah smiled. "Good. I do so hope this is just the beginning of our adventures together. I would hate it to be the end."

Zinnie was preparing to leave when the bell rang and the butler admitted Arthur Conan Doyle. He looked surprised and then pleased to see Zinnie.

"There you are!" he said. "How very fortuitous.

You were to be my next port of call."

"I was just leaving," Zinnie told him, edging towards the door. She had a feeling that, although Lady Sarah seemed happy to leave the events of the previous evening in the past, Conan Doyle had other ideas. "I have to get back. I told the girls I wouldn't be long."

"Then, my dear Lady Sarah, would you excuse me? With your permission, I will walk Miss Zinnie home and then come back again."

"Of course, Arthur," said Lady Sarah. "I shall be here, recovering from the exploits of yesterday evening."

CHAPTER 38

"I really don't need an escort," Zinnie said, as they left George Street and turned towards the Old Town. "It's far more likely to be the other way round."

"I know that," said Conan Doyle. "I just wanted to speak to you. Alone. You see, I have been thinking."

"Oh?"

"About last night."

"Oh."

"It seems to me," he continued, with the air of a man launching into what he expects to be a long explanation, "that while we may indeed have the spirits of the otherworld to thank for revealing both the murderer and his victim's whereabouts, there may also have been … other forces … at work."

"Other forces?"

"Of a more human nature," he added. "You see, here is what I've been thinking. That perhaps the interruption by the man called Talbot was not quite as much of a surprise as everyone thought, at least not to some of us."

"Well, no," agreed Zinnie. "MacDuff knew exactly what was going to happen because he set it up."

"That's true," said Conan Doyle. "But what if he wasn't the only person to know about that? That would mean that everything that happened thereafter – including the appearance of the *second* ghost – was not a surprise, either, at least not to those same people."

"But it was," said Zinnie. "You saw Aelfine – she was so scared that she fainted."

"Oh, of course, of course," said Conan Doyle. "I am just positing a possible second solution, that's all. If we are to question the notion of an *actual* ghost."

"All right," said Zinnie.

"Because it occurs to me," he went on, "that even if Aelfine had not been interrupted the first time, what is it that she would have said besides exactly what the 'real' ghost itself revealed? You see, here is my theory – if we are agreeing that there never was, in fact, a ghost in Mary King's Close."

"Except there was," Zinnie said. "You and I saw it, and other people did too. You *heard* it, Mr Conan Doyle, and declared yourself that it could be nothing but a ghost."

"Indeed. But indulge me, just for a moment. Imagine, if

you will, that someone enterprising had decided to stage a seance in order to reveal the identity of a murderer and the whereabouts of his victim's body. But that the blackguard had, in turn, learned of or at least suspected this plot and had taken steps to interrupt the so-called seance, intending to do so at the height of the subterfuge and therefore discredit his accuser and capture the culprit.

"What if this enterprising individual had decided that the way to turn the tide in her – or his – favour was to allow the seance to go ahead, even knowing that it would be ruined? What if that individual had then conspired to steal certain items, including some of the victim's possessions and also a small, intimate item belonging to the murderer? Say a set of clothes and a kerchief perhaps. The garments could be used to stage a second trick immediately in the wake of the first, in such heightened and stunning circumstances that no one present would believe it could possibly have been anything but real."

"But who would have performed the second trick?" Zinnie protested. "You yourself had hold of me and MacDuff had captured Aelfine! Who else was there?"

"Ah," said Conan Doyle, with a little shake of his stick. "Well, I should like to know exactly what time it was that young Miss Sadie actually arrived at the clinic after she left us on the Mile. Or indeed if that is where she went at all?"

Zinnie had no comeback for that. Conan Doyle gave a quick smile.

264

"The kerchief, meanwhile," he went on, "took a more gruesome route, namely to the body itself, as proof both of the murderer's identity and guilt. Then, when the spectacle unfolded and everyone was amazed, the truth would indeed seem as if it had come from beyond the grave. The murderer would be well and truly caught, and the victim finally laid to rest."

They had reached the entrance to Mary King's Close. Zinnie turned to Conan Doyle with a smile.

"You are so very clever," she said. "I could never have thought of that in a month of Sundays."

Conan Doyle looked at her with narrowed eyes. "I am not so sure of that, Miss Zinnie. I am not so sure of that at all." There was a slight pause and then he said, "You could have trusted me with the truth. I would have helped you and your sisters. All of them." He glanced the length of Writers' Court, his lips tightening in an unhappy line before he added, "I do understand why you did what you did, though, for Aelfine's sake."

Zinnie smiled again. "You're making things more complicated than they are, Mr Conan Doyle."

"And what is the simple solution?"

"That a restless ghost showed us the way to the body of a poor murdered woman."

Conan Doyle smiled. "Ah well," he said. "Perhaps, after all, the most obvious solution is the truth."

"That's usually the way," Zinnie said. "People like to

think the world more tangled than it is."

There was a pause, as if he were thinking carefully about what Zinnie had said. "Words to live by," Arthur Conan Doyle finally declared, with the definite air of a man putting a full stop to a sentence. "I will see you again, I am sure."

Zinnie scuffed the toe of her shoe against the ground. "Probably the next time you need help solving a mystery."

He laughed. "Of course, Miss Zinnie. Of that I have no doubt."

They said their farewells and went their separate ways, he back to the salons of the New Town, she to the underground recesses of Mary King's Close.

~EPILOGUE~

Two months later

"Nell, where are your shoes?"

"They're too tight! I don't like them!"

"That's because they're new," Zinnie called, as Nell charged back up the stairs with Aelfine and Ruby, all three of them shouting and laughing fit to lift the roof. "You need to wear them in, that's all! Aelfine's wearing hers! *Nell!* You can't be an explorer without shoes!"

"I'm not entirely sure that's true actually, dear," said Lady Sarah, her voice muffled as she struggled to pull a breastplate on over her riding habit. "I have heard tell of a particularly hardy people called Sherpas, some of whom can walk vast distances in the Himalayas wearing nothing on their feet at all."

There was a pause as she finally succeeded in yanking the stiff leather down over her chin. "Although I don't suppose that's much help in this instance. Nell!" she called. "If you don't put your shoes on, we can't go out and I had Cook use the last strawberries from the hothouse to make a cake especially for our supper expedition! It will have to be our last of the summer – you don't want to miss that, do you?"

The sound of the girls' footsteps stopped. There was an abrupt silence, broken just as suddenly by loud whispers. Then the three of them all thundered back down the stairs again, arriving in the entrance hall flushed and out of breath. It had been like this since the moment Nell, Aelfine and Ruby had met – together the three of them had become a whirlwind of frantic, inseparable friendship.

"That's better," said Zinnie. "Now, shoes on."

"I'll help you," Aelfine said, as Nell retrieved the offending articles. "It's easy once you know how."

Ruby chattered, grinning, as if to point out that *she* didn't have to wear shoes. Aelfine and Nell both stuck their tongues out at her.

"Where's Sadie?" Nell asked, as she sat on the bottom step of the stairs. "Isn't she coming too? And the doctor?"

"I should think so," said Lady Sarah. "Sadie is the keeper of the key, after all."

"We're here," came Sadie's voice, as she and Doctor Jex-Blake appeared out of the parlour that Lady Sarah had given over to Sadie for her studies.

"My goodness, Sarah," said Doctor Jex-Blake, seeing Lady Sarah's breastplate. "What on earth are you wearing?"

Lady Sarah looked down at herself, smiling broadly. "Fabulous, isn't it? I bought it from the sale of goods at the House of Wonders. I have a feeling it'll be perfect for our trip to South America. I'm testing it this evening to see how easy it is to move in – if it feels right, I shall have one made for Zinnie too."

The sale of MacDuff's ill-gotten gains had caused quite a stir, not just in Edinburgh but also further afield. Lady Sarah had bought quite a few pieces from his collection, including almost all the animals that he had penned up in those awful glass cases. Shortly after Ruby had come to Montague House, she had been joined by a mongoose, a porcupine and a capybara. Doctor Jex-Blake had persuaded her friend to draw the line at the boa constrictor, which had been taken instead to a zoo somewhere in England.

"It is really quite remarkable that so much wonder could come from such a terrible place, really," Lady Sarah went on. "Some on display and some … quite, *quite* hidden." She gave Aelfine an affectionate smile. "How lucky I was to find them at all. And now we really should get this expedition under way. It's getting late."

"We aren't carrying all this across to the gardens, surely?" Doctor Jex-Blake asked, looking at the bags and boxes in which Lady Sarah's cook, Martha, had diligently packed their supper picnic.

"Of course!" said Lady Sarah. "This is practice for Zinnie and I. Nell, my darling, how are you coming with those shoes? Ready to go yet?"

"I've got to bring Algernon! He needs a walk and some fresh grass!"

"Very well, but make sure you have his lead. I don't want to lose him again. And you'll have to carry him across the street. We can't have him getting squashed by a carriage, can we? Right, everyone," said Lady Sarah, as Nell went chasing off to find the tortoise. "Take hold of something to carry and we shall be off. Don't forget the blankets."

They were interrupted by the ringing of the doorbell. Zinnie opened it to find Arthur Conan Doyle standing on the doorstep in the early September sunshine. He had a copy of *Chambers's Journal* under one arm and a broad grin on his face.

"Miss Zinnie Montague!" he exclaimed, as she stood back to let him in. Then, "And my goodness – the entire household! Are you all off somewhere?"

"Arthur, dear boy, how good to see you," said Lady Sarah. "We are going into Queen Street Gardens with our supper. You will join us, won't you? I think we have enough to feed the five thousand."

"I would be delighted," said Conan Doyle. "After I have shown you … this!" He held up the magazine with a brilliant smile. It had been folded open to an inner page of narrow columns and a picture illustration beneath a curved title of elaborate letters.

"*The Mystery of Sasassa Valley*," Lady Sarah read aloud. "Oh! Is it your story, in print?"

"It is, indeed. I am not telling everyone, but you, my dear ladies, are of course the exception."

"Oh!" Lady Sarah said again, her voice thrilled as she took the magazine and examined the page. "May I keep this?"

"You may," said Conan Doyle. "I have another copy … or two…"

Lady Sarah went to one of the cabinets and pulled open a drawer, producing a pen and inkwell. "You must sign it, Arthur, for posterity's sake."

"Oh no, really," he said. "It'll probably be the only thing I ever publish."

"Pish," said Lady Sarah. "I am convinced that it is the start of a great literary career and so I insist." She dipped the pen in the ink and held it out to him, eyebrows raised.

"Oh, all right then," he said, with another grin.

"I shall look forward to reading it later," Lady Sarah declared, once he had scrawled his signature with a flourish above the title. "Now we must be away or we shall lose that beautiful late-summer light. Perkins, get the door, would you? Children, be careful of the street. Stay behind me."

Zinnie held back a moment, watching as Perkins held the door of Montague House open so that the faintly absurd procession could leave through it. Sometimes she still had trouble believing that she wasn't in some very strange, though wonderful, dream.

"I can read it to you," Conan Doyle said, moving to stand beside her. "My story, I mean. You might like it. It's full of adventure and strange goings-on. Right up your street, I should have thought."

Zinnie smiled. "Thanks, but I'll read it for myself."

"You are learning?"

"I thought I'd try again. It'll be useful for the expedition. And Lady Sarah has a whole library."

Conan Doyle smiled. "Ah yes, the expedition. How goes the planning?"

"Not sure yet," she said, hefting a bag of apples and cheese over one shoulder and catching up one of the blankets. "I'll let you know after supper. Come on – carry your weight. We're falling behind!"

She heard Conan Doyle laughing as she nodded good evening to Perkins and headed after her sisters, making for Queen Street Gardens.

Later, their supper consumed, the sun began to waver and dip over the townhouses of Edinburgh. Conan Doyle had taken his leave some time before, and now Zinnie watched as Aelfine and Nell played pirates with Ruby on the grassy slope below Sadie's neatly kept new flower bed. Lady Sarah had persuaded the groundsmen to give a patch of land over to plants of a purely medicinal nature. Sadie had overseen the planting and looked after it herself, and together she and the doctor were making a written record of their uses. Sadie was utterly engrossed in the endeavour. Even now she was sitting with her notebook, sketching the dark green leaves of a tall plant that bore white flowers.

A hasty truce was drawn up between the pirates and a moment later Nell and Aelfine came running towards Zinnie.

"Zinnie," Nell puffed, out of breath as she threw herself down on the blanket beside her big sister. "We've decided – we're coming to South America too. Aelfine and me. We don't care about the big spiders, or the bugs, or even the snakes."

Aelfine shuddered. "Maybe about the snakes," she gulped, eyes wide. "A little, *tiny* bit…"

Nell grabbed her hand, squeezing hard. "It doesn't matter about any of that," she insisted. "We're going to come even if we're scared, Zinnie. We're both really good sailors and swordfighters. You'll need us."

Zinnie smiled. This wasn't the first time the two youngsters had declared their intention to join the expedition.

"But what about Sadie?" Zinnie asked. "If you three come with us, she'll be all on her own."

"She can come too," said Aelfine. "We'll need a doctor."

"She's not a doctor yet. She must stay here to learn

how to become one. You three need to stay with her too, to keep her company and stop her getting lonely. Anyway, if you all come with us, who am I going to tell stories of my adventures to when I get back?"

"But we want to come with you!" said Nell, pouting. "We're sisters! We're supposed to stay together! We're supposed to look after each other!"

"Oh, pippin, give me a hug," Zinnie said. Nell threw her arms round Zinnie's neck. Zinnie held out her free arm and Aelfine curled into it. Sadie saw what was happening and put down her notebook and pencil, coming over to join in the hug. Zinnie, Nell, Sadie, Aelfine and Ruby the monkey, all holding on to each other in a silent pledge to never let go.

"We'll always come back together," Zinnie said. "No matter how far away we go, or where, or what we do. That's what sisters do."

"Sophia," Zinnie heard Lady Sarah murmur, as she and the doctor looked on. "I do believe that, given time, these girls could turn the whole wide world upside down all by themselves."

"We can but hope, my dear," said Doctor Jex-Blake. "We can but hope."

~AUTHOR'S~ HISTORICAL NOTE

Although this story is a work of fiction, there are a few aspects of it that are based on history. If you want to find out more about anything you read here, your local library will be able to help.

Mary King's Close and the other underground closes of Edinburgh still exist and you can visit them – the entrance is beside the Royal Exchange on the Royal Mile. You can take a guided tour that will explain more of the history of the site. There were actually people living in the semi-buried streets until the first decade of the 1900s, when the last shop finally shut and the family who owned it moved out.

Arthur Conan Doyle became, of course, the inventor of the modern detective novel with his stories about the uncanny deductions of Sherlock Holmes.

Fans of Holmes will know that the detective sometimes employs the talents of the 'Baker Street Irregulars' – a group of street children who know the city of London even better than he.

In 1879 Conan Doyle was 20, and a student at the Edinburgh Royal Infirmary. There he was taught by surgeon Joseph Bell, a doctor with a remarkable knack for using astute observations in his diagnoses – this would later become a hallmark of Sherlock Holmes's detective style.

In September of 1879, Conan Doyle had his first story published – *The Mystery of the Sasassa Valley*, a story about two young men discovering the truth behind the local legend of a ghost in Africa. The story was published anonymously and remained so until 1893, when an American edition added Conan Doyle's name to a reprint.

The supernatural had a huge influence on Conan Doyle's later life, and he became a firm believer both in the existence of ghosts and that there were mediums who could act as a conduit to the afterlife.

Sophia Jex-Blake lived during a time when it was difficult for women to have any career, let alone a medical one. When Jex-Blake decided she wanted to become a doctor, finding a university that would take female students was almost impossible. Eventually the University of Edinburgh allowed Jex-Blake and six other women to study there, but the women were met with opposition both from fellow male students and their tutors, which only escalated as they began to demonstrate that they were just as capable as their male counterparts. The hostility culminated in the 'Surgeons' Hall Riots' in 1870, when the women tried to attend an anatomy exam and were prevented by a violent mob of 200 people. The university then decided that the women would not be allowed to graduate, meaning that they would not be able to practice medicine. The women had to leave Scotland and go to other universities in England and America to obtain their medical degrees.

Jex-Blake finally received what she needed to be recognised by the General Medical Council in 1877. In 1878, in a stroke of defiance, she moved back to Edinburgh to open her practice, and became the first woman doctor in Scotland. Her first clinic was at 73 Grove Street, and she lived not far away at 4 Manor Place, where there is a plaque commemorating her residence. When her practice grew she moved to 6 Grove Street and established the Edinburgh Hospital and Dispensary for Women.

Jex-Blake later set up the Edinburgh School of Medicine for Women, which taught women from all over the world. She moved to Bruntsfield Lodge on Whitehouse Loan and when she retired the hospital moved into that site, the first Scottish hospital to be staffed entirely by women.

Isabella Bird is briefly mentioned as the inspiration for Lady Sarah's Hawaiian riding habit. She travelled all over the world alone, wrote many books about her journeys, pioneered travel photography (at one point washing her fragile glass photography plates in the Yangtze river in Asia) and became one of the first female fellows of the Royal Geographical Society in 1891. In 1869, though, she had taken a tour closer to home – to the tenements of Old Edinburgh, then wrote a pamphlet called *Notes on Old Edinburgh* in an attempt to raise money for better conditions. My favourite quote from it reads, "Bairns reared in such places are like lambs born among precipices – they early learn to take care of themselves." Sounds like Zinnie, doesn't it?

~ACKNOWLEDGEMENTS~

The history of Edinburgh is written into its architecture and it takes someone who knows the city inside out to read it properly. When I started researching *The House of Hidden Wonders* I contacted Robert Howie, who conducts historically focused walking tours of the Old Town. I asked if he could tailor one for me that centred on the Victorian period and he produced a brilliantly informative walk that provided me with a great background against which to write this story. He was also extremely generous with his own research materials and I will be forever grateful to him for his input. I thoroughly recommend one of his tours the next time you visit Edinburgh – his website can be found at www.historicedinburghtours.co.uk.

I am hugely grateful, as always, to my wonderful editors at Stripes, Ruth Bennett and Ella Whiddett. Thank you for always being so enthusiastic, thorough and caring – I have learned so much from working with you, and both of you have helped me to become a better writer.

The same goes, of course, for Ella Kahn, my agent at DKW, who always has an overwhelming amount of faith in my stories, for which I cannot express my thanks enough. Without you most of my ideas would be discarded before they even got to the page.

Huge thanks to Marg Hope who designed the wonderful cover and to Hannah Peck for the illustration – I've never seen my characters as images before and I love them. Thank you to Sarah Shaffi for the additional reading to help me with Aelfine and to Jane Tait for the (very thorough!) copyedit. Thanks also to Charlie Morris for her tireless efforts in publicising my books, and to the rest of the team at Little Tiger, each of whom are instrumental in getting a book like *The House of Hidden Wonders* on to the shelves. Thank you.

Last but never least, thanks to my ever-patient husband Adam Newell. While I wrote this book, he let me drag him all over Edinburgh multiple times; put up with having a huge print of a postal map of the city in 1879 hanging in our living room; waited for hours while I pored over photographs in the National Library of Scotland; used his expert skills as a second-hand bookhound to track down volumes for research; drove me two hours out of our way to find the only available copy of Shirley Roberts' biography of Sophia Jex-Blake – and that was on top of the usual downsides of being married to a naturally cantankerous author. Thank you, thank you, thank you.

Sharon Gosling is an award-winning writer who lives in Cumbria. Her first middle-grade book, *The Diamond Thief*, won the Redbridge Children's Book Award in 2014. Her young-adult horror title, *Fir*, was shortlisted for Lancashire Book of the Year 2017. *The Golden Butterfly* was nominated for the 2020 CILIP Carnegie Medal. She also writes books and articles about television and film, and has written, produced and directed audio dramas.

Sharon lives in a small fell village with her husband Adam, who has a second-hand bookshop in nearby Penrith. When she's not writing or reading, Sharon helps out in a café above the bookshop, makes art using a linocut set and creates jewellery.

@SharonGosling